TAMING OF THE SHOE

Also by
SARAH DARER LITTMAN

Charmed, I'm Sure

Fairest of Them All

TAMING OF THE SHOE

SARAH DARER LITTMAN

ALADDIN
New York   London   Toronto   Sydney   New Delhi

This book is a work of fiction. Any references to historical events, real people, or real places are used fictitiously. Other names, characters, places, and events are products of the author's imagination, and any resemblance to actual events or places or persons, living or dead, is entirely coincidental.

ALADDIN

An imprint of Simon & Schuster Children's Publishing Division

1230 Avenue of the Americas, New York, New York 10020

First Aladdin paperback edition August 2019

Text copyright © 2019 by Sarah Darer Littman

Cover illustration copyright © 2019 by Angela Navarra

Also available in an Aladdin hardcover edition.

All rights reserved, including the right of reproduction in whole or in part in any form.

ALADDIN and related logo are registered trademarks of Simon & Schuster, Inc.

For information about special discounts for bulk purchases, please contact Simon & Schuster Special Sales at 1-866-506-1949 or business@simonandschuster.com.

The Simon & Schuster Speakers Bureau can bring authors to your live event. For more information or to book an event contact the Simon & Schuster Speakers Bureau at 1-866-248-3049 or visit our website at www.simonspeakers.com.

Book designed by Laura Lyn DiSiena

The text of this book was set in Bembo Infant MT.

Manufactured in the United States of America 0719 OFF

10 9 8 7 6 5 4 3 2 1

The Library of Congress has cataloged the hardcover edition as follows:

Names: Littman, Sarah, author.

Title: Taming of the shoe / by Sarah Darer Littman.

Description: First Aladdin hardcover edition. | New York : Aladdin, 2019. | Sequel to: Fairest of them all. | Summary: Thirteen-year-old Araminta Robicheaux, Cinderella's daughter, embarrassed by her family, seeks to make her own fairy tale come true by showing her shoe designs to boy-band megastar Theo Downey.

Identifiers: LCCN 2019003805 (print) | LCCN 2019006627 (eBook) |

ISBN 9781534431584 (eBook) | ISBN 9781534431560 (pbk) | ISBN 9781534431577 (hc)

Subjects: | CYAC: Middle schools—Fiction. | Schools—Fiction. | Aunts—Fiction. | Bands (Music)—Fiction. | Characters in literature—Fiction. | New York (N.Y.)—Fiction. | Humorous stories. | BISAC: JUVENILE FICTION / Fairy Tales & Folklore / General. | JUVENILE FICTION / Humorous Stories. | JUVENILE FICTION / Family / General (see also headings under Social Issues).

Classification: LCC PZ7.L7369 (eBook) | LCC PZ7.L7369 Tam 2019 (print) | DDC [Fic]—dc23

LC record available at https://lccn.loc.gov/2019003805

To my beloved aunt, Barbara Garrison,
the first children's book illustrator I ever met

Chapter One

MY MOTHER IS TRYING TO RUIN MY LIFE.
Not only did we have to move to New York City for her business, but also she aired the commercial for her latest cleaning product, the Crud Crusher™, the night before I start at Manhattan World Themes Middle School. To top it off, it's halfway through the school year.

"Couldn't you have waited till I've been there a month or two before running that ad?" I asked.

"We're gearing up for the global launch, Araminta," Mom said. "Of course we couldn't wait."

"What's the big deal?" Dad asked. "It's just a commercial."

My parents are so clueless. They have no idea what it's like to be starting at a new school in the middle of the year, while bearing the surname Robicheaux, as in "House of Robicheaux, purveyor of superior cleaning products to royalty—and to you!"

If I could have legally changed my last name before I walked in the doors of my new school this morning, I would have done it in a heartbeat. Unfortunately, the law says I can't till I'm eighteen. Trust me, I checked last night after Mom's commercial aired.

It's one of the many reasons I'm hesitating outside the doors of my first class, social studies, wondering how long it will be before I'm outed as the daughter of Robert and Ella of Robicheaux. You probably know Mom by the name my two aunties came up with to torment her when they were all younger—that would be Cinderella.

Taking a deep breath, I walk into the room and approach the teacher, who my schedule tells me is named Mr. Falcone.

"Hi, I'm Araminta"—I whisper my last name— "Robicheaux."

"Aromatic Robot Shoe?" he says, looking very confused. I wonder if he's hard of hearing.

The kids who are already in the classroom start to laugh. I, however, do not.

"It's Robicheaux." I spell it for him, sotto voce, and I see a flash of recognition appear on his face.

"Ah yes, Araminta Robicheaux," he says. "You just moved here, correct?"

I nod. "Yes. Also, I prefer to go by Minty."

"I'll make a note," Mr. Falcone says.

"Robicheaux?" a guy sitting near the front of class says. "Are you related to the hot lady in the commercial? 'But wait, there's more! For just an extra nineteen ninety-nine plus shipping and handling, you can get the Soot Slaughterer. But that's not all! We'll throw in the Dust Decimator for no extra charge!'"

It's the first class in the first hour of my first day at this new school and I'm already known as my mother's daughter, thus slaughtering and decimating whatever chance I had of developing my own identity. Still, I can't help thinking this kid must watch waaaaay too much TV if he's got Mom's infomercial pitch memorized. Also, is he referring to *my mom* as "the hot lady"? *Eeeewwwwwwww!*

"Yes. She's my mother," I'm forced to admit. Why wasn't I born a better liar?

"I just saw an ad for the Crud Crusher last night!" a

girl says. "'Crush the crud that makes your castle a dud, with the Crud Crusher, from House of Robicheaux.'"

That makes two commercials, and I haven't even sat down yet.

"I saw your parents on *Barracuda Tank*!" a girl in the back says.

"I did too," Mr. Falcone says.

From the chorus of "me too" it sounds like most of the class did. Who knew that so many middle school students watched that show?

It was weird enough growing up seeing Mom doing infomercials. When I was little, I thought that everyone saw their parents when they turned on the TV. But things got really crazy after Mom and Dad went on *Barracuda Tank* last season. They emphasized the rags-to-riches (well, for Mom at least) and love-at-first-sight parts of their story. They played so well with viewers that their pitch segment got the highest ratings in *Barracuda Tank* history. The Barracudas totally ate up the fact that Mom took everything she learned when her stepmother and stepsisters turned her into an unpaid house servant and used her painfully acquired knowledge to create a successful line of cleaning products. The Barracudas love those pull-yourself-up-by-your-bootstraps stories. It didn't hurt that Mom's married to Dad, who just so happens to be a prince through accident of birth. As Barracuda Raymond Jack noted, "Royal titles are excellent marketing tools." All the Barracudas fought to give them the funding they needed to expand, but they ended up going with Tori Fournier, aka the queen of BSC, the Big Shopping Channel.

The products did so well on the Big Shopping Channel that Tori told my parents they should move the company headquarters from Robicheaux, the tiny kingdom ruled by my grandfather, to New York City to "facilitate the planned global expansion." At least that's the excuse my parents gave me for why I'm stuck starting a new school in the middle of the year.

"Take a seat, Miss Robicheaux, and share a book with the person next to you," Mr. Falcone says. "There's an empty desk in the back. I'll get a book for you tomorrow."

The back sounds perfect. I just want to blend in and feel normal, which isn't the easiest thing to do when the story of how your parents met is the subject of not just one but two romantic tales, and they've been on one of the highest-rated shows on television.

"You can share my book," the guy next to me says, pushing his desk closer to mine. "I'm Dakota." He's wearing a wool beanie on his dark curls, and a plaid flannel shirt with jeans. He's cute in an I-like-to-go-hiking-in-the-forest way.

"Thanks," I say.

Mr. Falcone starts talking about the causes of the War of 1812. I know a lot of this already because my grandfather Phillip, the king of Robicheaux, is obsessed with war strategy. He claims that learning about what causes wars, and how they were fought, is one of the keys to maintaining a peaceful kingdom. Since Robicheaux hasn't been involved in a war for more than three hundred years, he might have a point.

Dakota passes me a note.

I moved here this year too. So shout if you need anything.

I scribble on the paper and pass it back. As long as I don't do it in class :p

His lips twitch when he reads it. Probably a good idea ☺, he writes back.

When the bell rings for the end of class, Dakota asks me where I'm heading next. I look at my schedule.

"Math, with Mr. Kostek."

"I'll walk you there," he offers. "So you don't get lost."

"Thanks," I say. "So . . . how did you find it when you moved here?"

"Hard," he says. "I was used to living in the woods, in British Columbia. But then my dad got remarried."

"And your stepmother is from Manhattan?" I ask.

"No. Because of . . . well, some awkward family history, my aunt Gretel insisted that we—me and my sister—move to New York to live with her. And Dad didn't put up too much of a fight, so . . . here we are."

Something about this sounds familiar. *Living in the woods . . . a stepmother . . . the name Gretel . . .*

"Wait . . . is your dad . . . ?"

Dakota sighs, and then nods slowly. "Yeah . . . Dad's *that* Hansel and my aunt is *that* Gretel." He rubs the back of his neck. "As soon as Dad said he was getting remarried, Aunt Gretel flew out on the next flight to meet our stepmother-to-be. She brought us back to New York with her for our own protection."

I feel bad about having complained about my life. My parents might embarrass the heck out of me, but I can't imagine them giving me up without a fight. Maybe their dad is like the maternal grandfather I never met. He remarried after my grandma died, and let Horrible Hortensia the evil stepmonster treat Mom like a servant.

"Wow. That's rough," I say.

"It's been harder for my twin sister than it has been for me," he says. "She still has problems sleeping through the night because of the street noise."

"Yeah, the sirens really got to me the first night we were here," I confess. "But I just put in earbuds and listened to music."

A girl who looks vaguely familiar stops and says hi to Dakota.

"Hey, Aria," he says, stopping in the middle of the hallway. "This is Araminta."

"Please—Minty is less of a mouthful," I say.

"Minty it is," Dakota says. "It's her first day," he tells his friend.

That's when I realize who she is.

"Wait—you were on *Teen Couture*!" I exclaim. "You're Sleeping Beauty's daughter, right? You had the dog who pooped on the runway in the first episode! It was hilarious!"

Aria's cheeks turn rosy pink, even as she smiles. "For me, it's a lot more hilarious *in retrospect*," she says. "I wanted to sink through the runway at the time."

"Fair enough," I say. "Though I'd love to be on a show like *Teen Couture*. I love designing things. Specifically shoes."

"That's awesome!" Aria says. "You should come to Couture Club. Ms. Amara is great!"

"Just keep your needles away from Aria," Dakota warns. "She's got an unfortunate history."

"Very funny," Aria says. "Seriously, Minty, you should come to the meeting today after school."

"Yeah, it's fun," Dakota adds.

I'm surprised to learn that Dakota goes to Couture Club too. But then I wonder why I should be. Being able to design and make things you can wear is a practical skill that's probably even more useful in the woods of Canada.

You'd think I'd jump at the chance to go to a club that's about designing and making fashion—especially since the cutest guy I've seen at MWTMS so far goes to it too. There's a part of me that wants to go more than anything. But what Aria and Dakota don't know is that my step-aunties are in the shoe business. As much as I love clothes—especially shoes—it's yet another area where I feel it would be impossible to be my own person.

"I still have to finish unpacking," I say, even though that's not entirely true. Because of the suddenness of the move, I only got to bring one big suitcase of clothes from home. The rest of our stuff is coming at a later date.

"Oh well. Maybe next week," Aria says.

"I'll think about it," I say, careful not to make any promises.

By fourth period I've had people quoting Mom's infomercial at me in every single period at least once. I'm so sick of it. I get to English class early and find a seat in the back. I start sketching a cartoon about my first day at school to show Mom and Dad how bad it's been. You know, "a picture is worth a thousand words" and all that.

I look down at the cartoon I'm drawing, which so far has four frames of people singing me Mom's infomercials, with me getting more angry and upset in each frame until my head explodes all over the cafeteria. I'm using some artistic license, because lunch is next period.

I wonder how far away I'd have to move before I got to a place where no one had ever heard of my parents and House of Robicheaux™ cleaning products. Given that HOR is starting a global expansion, I'm starting to suspect it might be Mars.

I follow a few of the kids from my English class down to the cafeteria. After I get my food, I stand holding my tray, looking around at all the people who have their groups and places to sit. It makes me feel lonelier than ever. If I weren't my mother's daughter, I would take my lunch tray into the bathroom and eat in a stall, so as to not feel like such a loser. But when you've been brought up by the Queen of Clean, you know more than any sane person would ever want to about the hidden world of germy filth, especially in bathrooms. So I end up just standing there, feeling like the Girl Who Doesn't Belong.

That's until Aria taps me on the shoulder. "Are you looking for someplace to sit? Come join us!"

"I will. Thanks!" I say. I follow her to a table where two other girls are sitting.

"Sophie and Nina, meet Minty," Aria says. "It's her first day."

"Hi!" Nina says. "I was new here not so long ago. It gets easier."

There's something about her that looks really familiar. It takes me a second before I put two and two together.

"Are you by any chance Dakota's twin sister?" I ask.

"It depends. Did he do something dorky and embarrassing?" she asks.

"No, not at all," I assure her. "He was nice."

Cute, too, I think but don't say.

"In that case, yes, we're related," Nina says. "But I

reserve the right to revoke that if he's dorky."

"Minty—that's an interesting name," Sophie says. "Are you named after the herb?"

"It's short for Araminta," I tell her.

"That's so pretty," Nina says.

"I guess," I say. "But I've always wished that my parents named me something less pretentious."

A sudden shriek from a big table in the middle of the cafeteria makes me jump. A blond girl gets up and shouts, "Hunter! You got chocolate milk on my Seiyari-yashi Tomaki skirt!"

The guy she's yelling at is trying to apologize, but she's not having any of it.

"Do you know how much this skirt cost?" the girl shouts. "Five hundred dollars!"

"She paid five hundred dollars for a single skirt?" I gasp. "Wow. Things really *are* different in New York."

"Tell me about it," Nina says. "Why do you think I'm in Couture Club? Making my own clothes means I can actually afford to be fashionable."

"You can't judge everyone by Eva Murgatroyd's spending habits," Sophie explains. "Her parents are insanely rich. She's one of the 'popular people.'" Sophie uses air quotes, so I'm not sure if she means that or if she's being sarcastic.

"Yeah, getting an invitation to sit at her table at lunch is like being invited to a royal wedding," Nina says. Then she blushes. "But Aria, you've probably been to one."

"Believe it or not, I haven't," she says. "Mom and Dad avoid them—too many ceremonial swords. You know what freaks they are about sharp objects."

"I forgot," Nina says. "But I wish someone had been. I need a brain to pick about royal wedding fashion, because I want to design a fascinator for Aunt Gretel. She's obsessed with anything to do with royals. She practically lives on Charminglifestyles dot com. She reads every advice column Rosie Charming's mom writes about how to find a handsome prince."

If I weren't trying so hard to be my own person, I'd have told her I could ask my parents, since they had a very royal wedding. Their meet-cute was facilitated by help from either a fairy godmother or a magic bird, depending on which tale you read. Every time I've asked Mom which version of "How I Met Your Father" is true, she just laughs and says, "There's a little truth in both—it just goes to show that you shouldn't believe everything you read without considering the source."

I guess finding a handsome prince would be nice,

although, to be honest, the prince part doesn't matter to me as much as it does to my paternal grandparents. The qualifications of my ideal boy are as follows:

1. Handsome (obviously)

2. Smart (who wants to hang out with a guy who can't keep up?)

3. Funny (it's scientifically proven that laughter is good for you—it releases endorphins and fosters brain connectivity)

4. Not a frog or any nonhuman species. I don't believe the stuff I read in the tales that a frog can turn into a prince, even if it's kissed or thrown against the wall. A tadpole might turn into a frog, but a frog is still slimy and gross. Did you know a frog uses its eyeballs to swallow? #ewwwww #notkissable #science

By the end of my first day at Manhattan World Themes Middle School, I've added a new qualification. My ideal guy will never, ever, ever, *ever* quote one of my mother's infomercials to me when he learns my last name.

Chapter Two

MY MOTHER'S OBSESSION WITH DIRT IS BOTH
the bane of my existence and the key to her success. After
all those years when she was forced to sleep on the ashes
from the fireplace to stay warm in her father's drafty old
house, confronting the tiniest speck of dust or me leaving
my clothes on the floor of my bedroom upsets her equi-
librium. Big-time.

"How was the first day?" Mom asks. She's sitting at
the kitchen table with her laptop and a cup of tea, no
doubt working on some new marketing idea that will
make my life even more of a misery.

"I only had your new commercial sung to me by an

average of three kids per class," I complain, throwing my backpack down on the table. "But looking on the bright side, it could have been worse. I mean, they could have realized that I'm related to the aunties."

Aunt Margaux and Aunt Charlotte—known as Lottie—are my two step-aunts. They were the ones who tormented Mom by taking away her bed so she had to sleep in the ashes, and then made fun of her for being dirty by calling her Cinderwench and Cinderella. In other words, I have them and the evil stepmonster to thank for Mom's molysmophobia, which is a fancy way of saying that my mother is *seriously* freaked out by dirt.

For reasons I still haven't been able to figure out, Mom decided to forgive the aunties. Not only that, but she even made Dad appear with her in one of the infomercials for the aunties' unique line of Comfortably Ever After™ shoes.

"I would rather sentence them to trial by ordeal for how much they made you suffer," Dad said at the time.

Mom kissed him on the top of his head, where his princely hair is starting to thin a little.

"I appreciate the thought, darling, but you know what Charles Perrault said in his tale of our romance: 'Young women, in the winning of a heart, graciousness is more important than a beautiful hairdo,'" she told Dad.

It doesn't even make any sense. That Perrault guy literally spends the whole tale talking about how it was Mom's beauty that captured Dad's attention and made him so in *luuuuurve* that he was speechless and couldn't eat. Then Perrault ends the story by saying a beautiful hairdo isn't important? Talk about giving girls mixed messages!

At the time, we were learning about American history in school. "I'm pretty sure trial by ordeal counts as 'cruel and unusual punishment' under the Eighth Amendment to the Constitution," I told Dad.

"We don't live in America. We live in Robicheaux," Dad said. Then he suggested that I go to law school, since I like to argue so much.

"Speaking of the aunties, I've got news," Mom tells me now, putting down her brand-new I ♥ NY mug.

"What's that?" I ask, getting myself a package of fruit snacks from the pantry.

"Dad and I have to fly to Europe on Sunday for important meetings about the global expansion of House of Robicheaux. It's a last-minute thing—Tori Fournier is already there, and she set the whole thing up," Mom says. "Unfortunately, Granny Robicheaux is too busy arranging another charity ball to come stay with you while we're gone."

Dad's mother loves arranging balls. What normal person would come up with the idea of throwing a ball to which you invite every single young woman in your entire kingdom with the sole purpose of finding your son a wife? Granny Robicheaux, that's who. The show *The Bachelor* totally ripped off Granny R's concept, but it wasn't nearly as lavish. Her ball was like *The Bachelor* on steroids.

"Since Granny can't come to stay, I've asked the aunties to look after you while we're gone," Mom continues.

I choke on a strawberry fruit snack.

"You *whaaaaa?*" I wheeze when speaking is halfway possible. "Why would you do *that?*"

"Because they're the only ones I trust to be with you when Dad and I have to go to a different continent," Mom says.

It's a good thing I didn't put another fruit snack in my mouth before she said that, because I would be dying of asphyxiation right now.

"Are you *serious?* You can't find anyone else to whom you trust your beloved only child besides the ladies who threw lentils and peas into the ashes, made you pick them out, and then teased you because you were dirty?" I say.

"Araminta, that all happened once upon a time in a land far, far away," Mom says. "People grow. They can change."

That far, faraway land, Robicheaux, happens to be where I lived quite happily until my parents ripped me away from it in their fervent pursuit of World Cleaning Product Domination. I was one of the "popular people" there, like Eva "I spent five hundred dollars on a single skirt" Murgatroyd is here. But if I dare to point that out, I'll get another lecture about "opportunities for global expansion" and how "we're doing this all for you, Minty; money for college doesn't grow on trees."

I decide to take a different approach.

"Mom, Aunt Margaux cut off her own toes to try and fit into the glass shoe so she could marry Dad. Then Aunt Lottie tried to one-up her by cutting off her heel," I remind her. "That's not exactly the behavior of people who have all of their marbles intact."

"And because of their foot injuries, they were inspired to create the Comfortably Ever After line," Mom points out. "Now they are multimillionaires. They learned from their bad decisions. They turned lemons into lemonade."

"Their *self-inflicted* foot injuries," I mutter.

Mom looks at me from over the rims of her tortoise-shell reading glasses. "You could learn a lot from your aunties, Araminta, if you were more open to the idea."

The person who is supposed to be the most concerned with my well-being is leaving me with the women who tormented her, and now she's advising me to be "more open to the idea."

Someone is getting a BAD MOM T-shirt for Mother's Day.

"How long are you going for?" I ask.

"Just a week," she says.

"Just a week" with the aunties, right when I'm starting a new school. Ugh! I haven't even seen them in real life for, like, four years? It's bad enough having to see them on TV and know that we're step-related. Most of what I remember about the aunties is how loud they were, and how Dad and Grandpa and Granny Robicheaux looked at them like they were something dragged in from the stables on the bottom of a highly polished boot.

Just when I thought life couldn't get any worse . . .

"Why do you have to go *now*?" I ask. "You drag me away from my home and friends to a new city, and then you leave me here by myself. Actually, it's *worse* than by myself. You're leaving me with the aunties."

"I'm sorry about the timing, darling," Mom apologizes. "But when you're working to achieve a global product rollout, things crop up unexpectedly." She pats my hand comfortingly. "Besides, by the time we go, it'll be your second week of school."

"Like that's supposed to make me feel better?" I say, picking up my backpack and stomping down the hallway to my room. I kick off my shoes and leave them in the middle of the floor as a gesture of protest, and then put on my favorite band, Retro of Sync. Their lead singer, Theo Downey, is the best-looking person in the entire universe, although I will secretly admit that that guy Dakota in my social studies class is a pretty close second.

I take out my sketchbook and start working on a new shoe design. Yeah, I know, how predictable is it that I'm obsessed with shoes given my parents' life story? But I refuse to let accusations of predictableness interfere with my passion for fine footwear.

As I sing along to "A Million Miles to the Nearest Star," the new single from the latest Retro of Sync album, Theo's voice takes me to a place where life doesn't completely suck and my parents actually care about me instead of leaving me in the care of two weird ladies I haven't seen in years.

Still, when Mom calls me for dinner, I pick up my

shoes and put them in the closet. They don't deserve to be mistreated just because I'm mad at Mom.

Clearly, I stink at rebellion.

Dad brings home pizza for dinner. So far it's his favorite thing about New York. He groans with pleasure as he bites into a large slice, gooey with melted cheese. "They don't make pizza like this in back in the kingdom," he says. "Not even close."

"They say it's because of the New York water," Mom says. "Or because New York pizza parlors use older ovens that absorb the tastes and flavors. It's similar to using a well-seasoned skillet."

"Whatever the reason, it's yummy," I say, chewing on a crust. "By the way, Dad, you've got a big glob of cheese stuck in the dimple on your chin. You don't look all that princely when you're drooling mozzarella."

"You always look princely to me, Robbie," Mom says, gazing at him lovingly.

Barf. It's enough to turn a New York pizza lover off her dinner.

After our sumptuously cheesy repast, we're all sitting in the living room watching our new favorite reality show,

The Struggling Millionaires of Manhattan, when a commercial comes on for Comfortably Ever After™ shoes. Aunt Lottie is wearing a leopard-print outfit and black lipstick, Aunt Margaux is wearing a purple pantsuit with huge white sunglasses, and they're . . . attempting to rap. Kill me now.

> *If you think life sucks*
> *'Cause you didn't get the prince*
> *And your feet have got the blues,*
> *Don't you cry, 'cause you'll feel so fly*
> *In Comfortably Ever After shoes!*

Dad spits out a mouthful of his SleepyByes™ tea.

"Dad!" I exclaim. "Gross!"

"Ella, I think that's the most outrageous one yet!" he says, wiping tears of laughter from his eyes.

Mom's pretending to read, but she's turning red in the attempt to suppress her giggles.

It provides the perfect opening to question the combined parental wisdom of having the aunties look after me while Mom and Dad are away.

"So Dad—are you seriously on board with this plan to leave your precious, and I might add *only*, daughter with two rapping, tackily dressed lady bullies while you gallivant off to Europe with Mom?"

Dad pauses *The Struggling Millionaires of Manhattan*.

"'Gallivant off to Europe'?" he says, glancing over at Mom. "Ella, my love, you told me we were going on a work trip, so we can keep that precious *only* daughter of ours in the style to which she is accustomed."

"That's right, dear. It's going to be all work, work, work! Just like when I was a teenager in my father's house," Mom says with a chuckle.

One thing you should know about my mother: she plays the "When I was a teen, *my* life was *so bad*" card with me every chance she gets. It's super annoying, like I'm not allowed to think anything in my life sucks, ever, despite the fact that my parents just ruined it by taking me away from the only home I've ever known.

"Must we work, Ella?" Dad says. "Gallivanting sounds like much more fun!"

It's times like this I think my parents would have been better off without children. But like I said, my Robicheaux grandparents were so desperate to have a grandchild that they literally invited every single girl in the kingdom to a ball so Dad could pick a bride. According to the tale, Mom wowed Dad so much with her beauty that he "ate not a morsel" of the sumptuous feast my grandparents laid on, because "so intently was he busied in gazing on her." He also "never ceased his compliments."

"So basically he was a rich, princely creeper. Is that what you're telling me?" I asked Mom when I first heard Charles Perrault's version of how my parents met.

"It was better than listening to your aunts boss me around and call me Cinderwench all the time," Mom said. Then she laughed. "Besides, it's the only time I've ever seen your father willingly give up a chance to over-indulge on fine food."

As if on cue, Dad called out from the kitchen complaining that he had heartburn, and asking Mom where she'd hidden the antacids.

So it looks like I'm going to be stuck with the aunties for a week. I hope I survive. If not, "They lived happily ever after, but their daughter not so much" will make an interesting epilogue to my parents' tale.

The aunties arrive on Sunday morning, about an hour before Mom and Dad have to leave for the airport. My childhood recollection of them did not lie.

"Minty, darling!" Aunt Lottie shrieks loud enough to burst my eardrums as she hugs me to her bosom. "We're going to have so much fun together while your parents are gone!"

"'While the cats are away, the mice will play,'" Aunt Margaux says, winking.

I smile uneasily. Knowing the history, I'm worried it's more like the aunties are the cats who have plans to torment the mouse—in other words, me.

"Okay, I've left you our itinerary, the number of Minty's school, and the location of the nearest emergency room," Mom says. "You know, just in case."

The emergency room? If my parents are expecting me to come to ER-worthy bodily harm under my aunties' care, then why are they leaving me with them in the first place? I used to think they loved me. . . .

"Don't you worry about a thing, Ella," Aunt Margaux says. "We've got it all under control."

"We founded and run a multimillion dollar business," Aunt Lottie says. "How much trouble can one teenage girl be?"

Mom and Dad burst out laughing.

"More than you can ever imagine," Dad says between guffaws.

I am not amused.

"I'm not *that* much trouble!" I protest.

"Even if she is, we can handle it," Aunt Margaux says to reassure my parents.

"If worse comes to worst, we can make her pick lentils out of the hearth ashes as punishment," Aunt Lottie adds.

Everyone finds this incredibly hilarious—except for me. I resolve to put 911 on speed dial for the duration of my parents' trip. Fortunately, we don't have a working fireplace in this apartment, but knowing what I do of the aunties, I'm sure they can come up with creative new ways to make my life miserable.

Lottie and Margaux go to set themselves up in the spare room, leaving me alone to say good-bye to Mom and Dad.

"Are you one hundred percent sure you want to leave me alone with them for an entire week?" I ask them.

"You'll be fine, Minty," Mom assures me, hugging me and kissing my forehead. "How many times do I have to tell you? Margaux and Lottie have *changed*."

As I watch the elevator door closing, taking my parents downstairs to get the car to the airport, I wonder just how much.

Chapter Three

"ARAMINTA! ARE YOU READY? WE'RE GOING
to walk you to school," Aunt Margaux says from the
doorway of my bedroom the following morning. Aunt
Lottie is standing right behind her, grinning like a color-
fully dressed Cheshire cat.

I've just finished trying on the third outfit in ten
minutes, in what seems like a futile attempt to capture
a New York fashion vibe. After seeing how fashion-
forward Aria Thibault and Eva Murgatroyd are, I'm
trying to up my game. I might have to give Couture
Club a try after all.

At least my footwear is on point: my treasured Trudy

Neal ballet flats, which are silver with purple soles and fit me perfectly. I saved up to buy them as soon as I saw them in the vintage clothing store, because it's hard to find cool shoes when you have really small feet like I do.

Right now I've got a more immediate problem to deal with. "What do you mean, walk me to school?" I ask Aunt Margaux. "I'm thirteen years old. I walk myself to school."

"Not on our watch," Margaux says. "We're responsible for keeping you alive and in one piece until Ella and Robbie get back. We're not taking any chances."

"But Mom and Dad have been letting me walk to school alone!" I protest. "This is New York City!"

"Exactly my point," Margaux says. She smiles. "Besides, we have a surprise for you."

"Margaux!" Aunt Lottie snaps. "You weren't supposed to say anything!"

Usually I'm okay with surprises, but the thought of one involving the aunties makes me *very* nervous.

"What kind of surprise?" I ask, grabbing my backpack.

"If we tell you, it won't be a surprise, silly!" Aunt Lottie says. She checks the time on her Flitbit. "Come on, we need to leave now or we'll be late."

Despite my multiple wardrobe changes, there's still

plenty of time to get to school. She must mean late for the surprise.

I hope it's food-related. Maybe they're going to take me to Patisserie Bon Gateaux and buy me some delicious cupcakes.

But alas, we walk straight past the patisserie.

When we're a block away from Manhattan World Themes, I notice that there are barricades in front of the building, and a bunch of trucks. One of them has SOUP TO NUTS CRAFT SERVICES in big letters on the side.

"I wonder what all those trucks are there for."

"That's the surprise!" Aunt Lottie shouts in my ear, beaming with excitement. "We're filming a commercial for our new line of shoes, Comfortably Ever After for Youth, *right here at your school*!"

"And all your friends can be in it!" Aunt Margaux adds, waving a beringed finger at the scene across the street.

I am officially dead.

"This is literally my fourth day at this school. I haven't got that many friends," I say. "And after this, I'm never going to!"

"Don't be such a drama queen, Araminta," Aunt Margaux says. "*Everyone* wants to be on TV. I guarantee you're going to be embraced by the most popular kids at this school by the end of the morning."

"Trust us on this," Aunt Lottie says, patting my arm in an attempt to comfort me.

Trust *them*? Let me think. . . . *No!*

But then I notice how many students are crowding around the police barriers. The whole corner is buzzing with excitement.

We cross the street, and the aunties go straight over to the barriers.

"We're filming a commercial for our new youth line of comfort sneakers," Aunt Lottie announces. "Would anyone like to be in the ad?"

The shouts of "Yes!" and "Me!" and "Woo-hoo!" and "Yes, please!" are so loud they drown out the street traffic.

"Great!" Aunt Margaux says. "Just line up and check in with our lovely production assistant Marco. As long as your parents sign the photo release, you can be in the commercial. No photo release, no go. It's the law."

"Oh, that's too bad," I say, relieved. "I can't be in it because Mom and Dad are out of the country, and they didn't sign a release."

"Nonsense!" Aunt Lottie says. "Margaux and I are acting *in loco parentis* while Ella and Robbie are away."

I assume that means "like a crazy parent" until I look it up on my phone and find it's a Latin legal term for "in the place of parents."

"But it'll make us all late for school!" I say. "How popular will I be if everyone in school ends up with a detention because of this?"

"Don't worry about that," Aunt Lottie assures me. "We cleared everything with your school principal, Mr. Hamilton. He sent out the photo-release forms and asked parents to keep the whole thing a secret until this morning."

Aunt Margaux cackles loudly. "It's amazing what a six-figure donation to the school can accomplish—right, Lottie?"

I've learned two things this morning before I've even walked through the school door: (1) My principal, Mr. Hamilton, is easily bought, and (2) there's no escape from the aunties. I'm going to have to be in this commercial no matter what.

The strange thing is, all the kids around me are super excited about it. Is Aunt Margaux right that everyone wants to be on TV?

Two guys wearing MWTMS SOCCER hoodies come over.

"Right on!" Quinn says. He's the guy from my social studies class who called Mom "the hot lady." In other words, he's gross and I've been trying to avoid talking to him if at all possible.

The other one, who I think is the Hunter who spilled chocolate milk on Eva Murgatroyd's insanely expensive skirt, says, "Thanks for getting us out of first period." He raises a fist, which he obviously expects me to bump.

"Uh, my pleasure," I say, figuring the best thing I can do is go with the flow. I tap his knuckles lightly with my fist.

Maybe I should trust the aunties. Maybe they're right. Maybe this won't be a total social disaster.

Then Eva Murgatroyd comes over. She's wearing a cute skirt and I wonder if it cost five hundred dollars like the chocolate-milk one.

"Hi!" she says, with a big smile. "You're Araminta, right? Your aunts said that it's because of you we get to be in the commercial."

They did?

"Oh. Yeah," I say, hoping that they really said it and she's not just testing me. "They were looking for extras and I suggested that they film it here, because it's for a new youth line of shoes and we're 'youths.'"

Eva laughs. "Your aunts said they wanted to film here because we're so obviously sophisticated."

The aunties are lying up a storm, but it seems like Eva is buying what they're selling. No wonder they're multimillionaires.

"Can you get me free shoes?" Eva asks. "I'm an influencer on social media and I can post pictures of me wearing them on Pinstagram to boost sales. Seiyariyashi Tomaki just *loves* what I do."

I take it back. She's not buying what the aunties are selling. Does this mean she didn't actually pay for the five-hundred-dollar skirt?

Since Lottie and Margaux are lying to help me, I decide to return the favor.

"Sorry. I'm not allowed to do that. The aunties are strict about freebies," I tell Eva. "Even *I* don't get free shoes."

That's because I wouldn't be caught dead wearing them, but Eva doesn't need to know.

"Too bad," Eva says. "Well, I'll be over there with Hunter, Quinn, and Ginny."

Apparently she's forgiven Hunter for the Chocolate Milk Incident.

A woman with a clipboard and a megaphone introduces herself as Aayesha and says that she's going to divide us into two groups. Each group is going to dance behind a different auntie. A select few, who have the right shoe sizes, will be in front, each of them wearing a different style from the new Comfortably Ever After™ for Youth line.

"If I call your name, come to the first trailer and get your shoes," Aayesha says.

Luckily, I have super-small feet, so there's no way they're going to have my size. If I can hang out in the back of the crowd, with any luck my face won't be visible.

"Araminta Robicheaux, size four."

Ugh! Just my luck. The aunties must have gotten my shoe size from Mom, who apparently hates her only daughter.

Dreading what I'm going to have to put on my feet, I walk over to the first trailer as Aayesha announces the rest of the unfortunate shoe wearers.

"These are your size," the person in the trailer says, handing me a pair of what look like a cross between Mary Janes and sneakers, with platform heels. All of this in a patchwork of clashing colors. They're ugly squared.

I sit down on one of the chairs in the trailer and take off my vintage Trudy Neal flats, unable to believe I have to put these awful-looking things on my feet.

Unfortunately, they fit. Perfectly. Almost like the aunties took a plaster cast of my feet while I was asleep. I wouldn't put it past them.

Eva Murgatroyd is another chosen one. She shrieks when she sees the shoes she's been allotted, which are neon green with shocking pink leopard spots. Their soles are silver, and they sport neon-yellow laces.

"Livvy, look at these!" she says. "I need sunglasses so I won't be blinded by them!"

"I *love* mine," her friend Livvy says. She's lacing a pair of shiny gold sneakers with glitter soles and silver sparkle laces onto her feet. Hers definitely aren't as awful as Eva's.

When I stand up, I realize that while the shoes on my feet are supremely ugly, they are also exactly what the aunties promise in their ads—super comfortable. Way more comfortable than any of the shoes I have in my closet. I hate to admit it, but they're even more comfortable than my Trudy Neal flats. If only I could persuade the aunties to make them less . . . *hideous*.

As I exit the trailer, I bump into Dakota, who is another lucky winner.

"Good luck," I tell him.

He looks down at my feet and starts cracking up.

"Those are . . . something. I just don't know what, exactly."

"Ugly?" I suggest.

"I didn't want to insult your aunts, but yeah, that pretty much covers it," he says, his dark eyes alight with amusement.

"I know. But they're super comfortable," I say. "So at least there's that." I smile at him. "Can't wait to see what *you* end up wearing."

What Dakota ends up with is a pair of chunk-wedge sneakers in bright orange, with peace signs on them.

But we don't get to commiserate for long, because Aayesha the Megaphone Lady starts dividing us into two groups. Then she introduces Shana, the choreographer, who teaches us how we're supposed to dance down the sidewalk behind the aunties. She makes us practice it a few times to make sure we've got it right.

Dakota is a natural. Me . . . not so much.

"You in the patchwork Mary Janes—you're clapping on the wrong beat!" Shana shouts through the megaphone.

I might be good at many things (none of which I can actually think of at the moment), but clapping on the beat and dancing at the same time is not one of them.

Shana makes me practice all by myself in front of every-one, because I'm apparently the only front-row person who lacks coordination.

As I hear all the laughter, I decide the likelihood that Aunt Margaux is right and this commercial is going to be good for my social life is now less than 50 percent. I would start praying for an earthquake to swallow me up and end this torture, but there's no way I can dance, clap on the beat, *and* pray. Instead I flush to a temperature that I'm sure is unhealthy and wonder if it's possible to literally die from embarrassment.

"Okay, we're going to try a take," Aayesha says when Shana declares me "just about passable."

The aunties come out of their trailer. Aunt Lottie is wear-ing red leather pants and Aunt Margaux is wearing black ones. They're both wearing black T-shirts that say OLD BUT RAD! and shoes from the Comfortably Ever After™ adult range that give a new definition to hideous. I groan loudly, but the cheering from my fellow students drowns me out.

What am I missing? Why does everyone else think this is so awesome?

I wonder that even more after the first take, during which the aunties sing a new rap as we dance behind them on the sidewalk:

It's time, my youths, let's hear ya holla
Here with all these hip young scholars.
Lottie and Margaux gonna drop some knowledge
'Cause ya know ya gonna wanna go to college.

Don't just stand there like a bystander—
The sistahs are here to dish with candor.
If ya got sore feet, ya can't think in school
Can't learn the three Rs or the Golden Rule.

Our shoes are the very things you need
'Cause you don't want your toes to bleed.
What else would you put on your poor feet?
Gotta love it, the sisters speak for the street.

Comfortably Ever After for Youth Shoes:
Try 'em—otherwise you're a fool.

HOLLA!

After listening to that "rap," I lower the chance of Aunt Margaux being right about this making me new friends to less than 10 percent—most likely zero. I wonder if I can transfer to another school. I make a mental note to look into that when I get home.

We do five takes, and then Aayesha shouts, "And that's a wrap!" through her megaphone. Then she hands the megaphone to the aunties.

"You were all wonderful extras," Aunt Lottie says.

"As a thank-you, you each get a *Comfortably Ever After* T-shirt from the new youth range," Aunt Margaux says, holding up a T-shirt that says YOUNG AND GLAD!

Marco hands the aunties T-shirt cannons and they start shooting T-shirts into the crowd of MWTMS students. Unfortunately, Aunt Lottie isn't very good at aiming, and one goes into the middle of the intersection. It lands on the windshield of a taxi, which startles the driver, causing him to swerve and hit a bus in the next lane, with a loud crash of crushed metal and shattering glass.

"Oops," Aunt Lottie says.

"Lottie, I *told* you to let me do the T-shirt cannons," Aunt Margaux says. "You've always had lousy aim."

"What are you talking about?" Aunt Lottie shouts. "I always got the lentils into the fireplace when we were throwing them for Ella to pick out. Yours ended up all over the kitchen floor!"

While the aunties launch into a massive argument, the taxi driver gets out of his car, picks up the T-shirt, and looks around. He spots the aunties holding T-shirt cannons and walks toward them, shaking his fist and using words that would get me grounded.

"Okay, students, back in the building!" Mr. Hamilton shouts. "NOW."

"But Mr. Hamilton, I didn't get my free T-shirt yet," Eva complains.

I thought Sophie said Eva's parents were crazy rich. So why does she seem to want everything for free?

"We'll get them to you," Mr. Hamilton says. "Now get inside."

I want to go inside more than anything, but I'm also worried about the aunties' safety, even though they are two of the most embarrassing people who bear some relation to me.

As the taxi driver approaches them, calling them all kinds of names and making threats, Aunt Margaux says, "Stop right there, sir." She and Aunt Lottie point their T-shirt cannons at his chest. "We are more than happy to compensate you for any damage to your vehicle, but we'd appreciate if you refrain from curse words. There are children present."

She speaks calmly and doesn't show any fear. For the first time, I feel a flicker of pride that we're related, even if it is from the marriage of the grandfather who died before I was born to their mother, Horrible Hortensia.

Aunt Lottie sees me watching. "Go on in, Minty, dear," she calls to me. "We've got this under control."

I give her a thumbs-up, say, "I'll see you after school," and turn to go into the building. I almost bump into Eva Murgatroyd, who is standing right behind me.

"That was so cool," she says, grinning from ear to ear. "Your aunts are the bomb."

I can't tell if she's joking or serious. But then she links her arm in mine and starts pulling me toward the school entrance.

"I've always wanted to be on TV," Eva says.

"I guess it's your lucky day?" I say, thinking how weird it is that she's acting like we're BFFs all of a sudden.

"It's *your* lucky day too," she says. "Because *you* get to sit at my table at lunch."

I readjust the probability of Aunt Margaux being right about improvements to my social life to 100 percent. After all, according to Sophie, Eva is one of the *popular people*.

"Thanks!" I say. "I'm pretty new to Manhattan World Themes."

"Just sit at my table for lunch for a few days with the rest of Eva's Elites and you'll know *everyone*." She shrugs. "Well, at least everyone who matters."

Wait . . . doesn't everyone *matter?*

I don't say it, because I'm still new and I don't want to jeopardize my chance to sit at her table and meet people.

"Thanks," I say instead. "I'll see you later."

I thought that eventually I'd be able to escape hearing imitations of commercials by my relatives in every single class period of every single day, but that's definitely not going to happen anytime soon, thanks to the aunties. Everywhere I go, someone is either wearing a YOUNG AND GLAD! T-shirt or waiting to give me their best rendition of the aunties' awful raps. Even when I go to the restroom between classes, a girl starts singing, "'Lottie and Margaux gonna drop some knowledge / 'Cause ya know ya gonna wanna to go to college'" from the next stall. If I survive my parents' trip to Europe with my sanity intact, it will be a bona fide miracle.

Still, I'm nervous about sitting with the "popular people" at lunch. I see Nina, Sophie, and Aria at the usual table and wonder if I should go sit with them instead, but

Eva spots me and shouts: "*ARAMINTA!* Come sit next to me!"

I walk over and put down my tray at the place that Eva has apparently been saving for me. As I do, I glance over to where my other new friends are sitting and meet Nina's quizzical gaze. I shrug and smile at her as I take my seat next to Eva. Nina says something to Aria and Sophie, who turn in my direction. They seem . . . disappointed.

When I sit down, I recognize Quinn from social studies and his friend Hunter Farthington, and this girl Ginny Krulinsky who is in my English class. There's also Eva's friend Livvy and a guy who tells me his name is Connor Henderson.

"Those were Araminta's aunts outside filming the commercial this morning," Eva says. "I'm in it!"

"Please, call me Minty," I say.

Hunter does a really poor imitation of one of my aunts' previous commercials:

"'When life hands you lemons, you make lemonade. / If you cut off your toes, your feet need some aid. / So check out our line of comfortable shoes. / Trust Margaux's feet— you'll be glad that you do!'" he sings in a painful falsetto.

Ugh. Like I haven't heard this, like, fifteen times already today, and it's only lunch.

Forcing a polite smile, I say: "You're almost as good a singer as my aunties."

It's not a compliment, but he takes it as one, turning to high-five Quinn. I get the impression Hunter isn't one of Manhattan World Themes Middle School's leading intellectual lights.

Luckily, the conversation turns to other topics besides my embarrassing aunts and their even more embarrassing ads.

"Less than a week till Retro of Sync!" Livvy squeals. "I can't wait!"

"Wait—they're playing in New York?" I ask. "I can't believe I'm in the same city and don't have tickets."

I wonder if I can ask for an early birthday present. Oh, wait, my parents are off gallivanting in Europe, so I can't.

"My dad got tickets for me and a friend. That's the only reason Livvy is going," Eva says.

Livvy's irritation flashes over her face for an instant—until she turns to me.

"You're a Synco too?" she says, using the name ROS fans call one another.

"They're number one on my playlist," I say. "I love their lyrics—and Theo Downey is super cute."

"Well, don't get any ideas—he's mine," Eva says. "And besides, the concert is sold out."

I consider pointing out that part of Theo's magic is that every single person who listens to him singing "You're My Only Dream Girl" thinks it's being sung to her and only her, but Eva continues, "And I'm going to meet him while he's in New York if it's the last thing I do."

"Eva keeps coming up with wacky plans to get into their hotel and sneak up to Theo Downey's room," Livvy explains.

"They're not wacky!" Eva protests. "You're just jealous because Theo loves me."

Connor laughs. "I'll bet you any money that Theo Downey doesn't even know you exist," he says.

"How much do you want to bet?" Eva says.

"I'll buy you a cookie," Connor says.

Eva takes out her phone, opens Pinstagram, and goes to favorites. "You owe me a chocolate chip, then," she says, showing her phone to Connor. "Theo liked my Pin."

Connor laughs even harder, joined by the rest of the table. "The guy has, what, like a million followers? Do you think he even responds to his own Pinstagram?"

I agree with Connor, but I'm not about to say so, because Eva was the one who invited me to sit here. A pinkish flush is rising up her neck into her face.

"You just want to get out of buying me a cookie," Eva says. "So much for integrity!"

"It's not that," Connor says. "Just because he liked a Pin doesn't mean he knows who you are."

"You didn't say that," Eva points out. "You said he doesn't even know I exist. He liked my Pin, so he knows I exist."

I remember Dad quoting me some philosopher, what was his name . . . Descartes? He said, "I think, therefore I am." Today Descartes would probably say, "He liked it, therefore I exist" instead.

Eva lifts her chin and tells Connor, "There. I proved it. You owe me a cookie."

"Ha-ha!" Hunter says. "She busted you, dude."

"No, she didn't!" Connor protests. "That's just—"

"A bet's a bet," Eva says. "Now pay up and buy me a cookie."

"Wait, we should vote on it," Connor says. "You and I can't vote because it involves us. But everyone else should."

"Fine," Eva snaps. "Who thinks I'm right?"

Ginny and Livvy raise their hands.

"And who thinks *I'm* right?" Connor asks.

Hunter and Quinn raise their hands.

"Looks like it's a tie," Livvy says.

"Minty didn't vote!" Eva says. "Come on, Minty, you're the tiebreaker."

Great. I purposely tried to stay out of it to be diplomatic, and now I have to be the one to break the tie. Then I get an idea for how to save the situation.

"Uh . . . I think Connor should buy Eva a cookie," I say. Eva flashes Connor a triumphant look. "But then she should split it with him."

"What?" Eva exclaims. "Why?"

"Well . . . you're right on a technicality, but I think Connor's right about the other thing," I say, wondering if this is going to be the end of my brief whatever-not-quite-a-friendship-yet with Eva.

A second or two passes, and I'm sure she's going to tell me that I've failed the Eva's Elites entrance test and I'm an ungrateful not-quite-a-friend-yet, but then she shrugs and says, "Fair enough. I'm happy to prove all you wrong when Theo and I meet." She smiles at Connor. "So how about that cookie?"

"Yeah, okay," he says, pushing back his chair. "But only because I'm getting half."

Eva and Connor go off to get the cookie. "Well played," Livvy says. "Very wisdom-of-Solomon."

She means King Solomon, who, when confronted by two women each claiming that they were the mother of a baby, said they should cut the baby in half and each take a share. He knew who the real mother was because she would rather the other woman get the baby then have it come to any harm. Smart guy.

I smile and shrug. "My dad says I should go to law school."

I don't tell her that it's because I argue so much.

Livvy asks me what kind of things I enjoy doing. "Basically, I'm all about shoes," I say. "I love designing them . . . and buying them, of course."

"Oh, so maybe you can work for your aunts some-day," Livvy says.

Ugh. That would be a total nightmare. "Yeah . . . not so sure about that. We have very different . . . styles."

"Their shoes are a little out there, but they were super comfortable," she says. "What kind of shoes do you design?"

There are few things I enjoy more than being able to show people my designs—well, unless those people are related to me, that is. I whip out my sketchbook and show Livvy some of my latest sketches.

"Wow, you're so talented," she says. She points to the block-heel, music-themed Mary Janes I dreamed up last week while Theo Downey's voice calmed my parental-induced anger. "I love these!" Then she claps her hand to her forehead. "Omigosh! The competition! You should totally enter it!"

"What competition?" I ask.

"The one to win tickets to the Retro of Sync concert!" she says. "The person who does the best shoe designs for each of the band members based on a ROS song wins a VIP box at the opening show of the tour in New York."

Excitement fizzes in my veins at the thought I could possibly get tickets to see my favorite band in the whole universe. "I'm definitely going to enter!"

Livvy bites her lip. "I just hope it's not too late. The concert is on Saturday night."

I take out my phone, and I'm about to look it up when Eva and Connor get back, each clutching their half of a cookie.

"Eva, do you know the deadline for the ROS design contest?" Livvy asks her.

"Why would I enter that? I've already got tickets," Eva says.

"It's not for you. It's for Minty," Livvy says. "Minty, show Eva your designs!"

I push my sketchbook across the table, and Eva leafs through my shoe sketches.

"Not bad," she says slowly.

That's when I see on the ROS website that the deadline for the contest was . . .

"Oh no. I'm too late. The deadline was yesterday."

Talk about raising, then crushing my hopes. If I'd known about this twenty-four hours ago, I could have been a contender.

Livvy sees the devastated look on my face. "I'm so sorry, Minty," she says. "If I'd known the deadline had already passed, I wouldn't have said anything."

"It's okay," I say, even if I feel decidedly not okay. But that's not Livvy's fault.

"They haven't announced the winners yet," Eva says slowly. "Let me think about it. Maybe there's a way to get your designs to Theo Downey, even if the deadline has passed. After all, Daddy has lots of connections and I'm a social-media influencer, so . . ."

I don't know how those things help if the deadline has

already come and gone, but I'm so desperate to see the show I'll try anything.

"That would be great!" I say, hope fluttering like a butterfly in my chest.

"You know, Livvy's coming over to my house tomorrow after school," Eva says. "You should come too."

"Uh, sure!" I say, curious what a crazy-rich person's apartment looks like.

"Maybe I'll have figured out a plan by then," she says. Then she gives me a speculative look. "In the meantime, you can ask your aunts about the free shoes."

I should have known there would be a catch. But still, if Eva can help me get my designs to Theo so I've got a chance of winning tickets to the sold-out concerts, it will be worth it.

Chapter Four

BY THE END OF THE SCHOOL DAY, I'M CON- vinced my head will explode if I hear another person sing me one of my aunties' awful raps. It's only my second week at this school and my identity has already been defined by my family's advertising jingles. How am I ever going to be my own person?

The thought of going back to the apartment and being with the aunties is more than I can take. I need time away from my family and its legacy.

I've overheard people at school talking about a coffee shop called Starcups, so I decide to head there instead.

The aroma of roasted beans hits me as soon as I open

the door. I recognize a few kids I've seen at school, but I'm not in a mood to talk to anyone from MWTMS, because they'll probably start singing: "'Comfortably Ever After for Youth Shoes: / Try 'em—otherwise you're a fool.'" Then I'd be tempted to take the tea I'm lining up to buy and pour it over their heads. While I'd finally be known for something I did myself instead of something to do with my family, I don't want that something to be because I've been arrested for being a deranged hot-beverage pourer.

I'm definitely better off sitting alone. The problem is, the place is so crowded that once I've purchased my Starcups Passionflower Tea ("Promotes a more balanced mood!"), there's only one vacant chair left in the place, near the window, where a woman dressed in purple is already sitting. I go over to her and ask, "Is this chair free?"

"Nothing in life is free, baby," she says. "But you go on and take a seat."

"Thanks," I say, noticing that she has delicate purple highlights in her hair, and her nails are long and done with silvery polish with a hint of sparkle. If I dressed head to toe in purple, I'd look like a human grape, but she pulls it off. The color brings out her amber eyes and complements her dark skin. She's got a book in her lap, and she's wearing a pair of bright turquoise reading glasses.

I settle into the chair and pull out a notebook and pen, planning to make a start on my homework. But as I take a few sips of my tea, this morning's mortification keeps replaying in my mind, and I wonder if I will ever live down being on television wearing those ugly (although admittedly super-comfortable) things on my feet.

If only the aunties made shoes that were that comfortable but actually looked good. I bet that's what Theo Downey would want to wear during a performance.

My hand starts moving as if by its own accord, pulling my sketchbook and a pencil out of my bag. Instead of working on the essay I'm supposed to be writing about the Emancipation Proclamation, I start coming up with ideas for the shoes I would have entered in the Retro of Sync VIP concert-ticket competition—if I'd only known about it before the deadline.

"You really like to draw, huh?" the woman in purple says, lifting up her readers and leaning across the table to look at my sketch.

I stop sketching. "Yes. How did you know?"

"Because you were wound up like a spring when you sat down, and as soon as you started drawing that shoe, I could feel the tension drift out of your body," she says.

At first I think she's talking what Grandpa Robicheaux

would call "earthy-crunchy mumbo jumbo," but then I realize that I *am* feeling better than when I walked in.

"It's probably the passionflower tea," I say.

"Except you've barely touched yours," she says.

I glance at my mug of tea and realize that she's got a point.

"So what had you so wound up?" the lady asks.

"My family," I blurt out before remembering that I don't even know this woman's name, much less who she is, so I probably shouldn't be telling her everything that's wrong with my life.

"People like to tell me their problems," she says, like she just read my mind. "I'm a good listener." She smiles. "It's my job to help people be their best selves and achieve happiness."

"Are you some kind of therapist?" I ask.

She bursts out laughing.

"Not exactly. But it ends up being part of the job." She leans forward, putting her elbows on her knees. "So go on and tell Leila what's got you so riled up."

At least I know her name now, and there's something about her that makes me want to spill.

"I wish I could be my own person. I want to be known for something *I* do instead of what my relatives have done," I say with a sigh. "But right now it feels like it's never going to happen."

"Never say never, Minty," she says. "You can't know what the world has in store for you."

"You don't know my family," I say, shaking my head. "They cast a big shadow."

Leila chuckles, as if what I said was the punch line to a joke only she knows. Then she looks out the window and smiles. I follow her gaze and see people hurrying by on the sidewalk. Then I see a small bird sitting on a parking meter just outside the cafe, its head cocked to one side as if it's listening to our conversation.

Stress must be getting to me. I'm starting to think a bird is spying on me.

"Not only that—I'm desperate to go to the Retro of Sync concert, but it's all sold out," I tell her. Then I point to the shoe sketch. "I could have entered a contest to design shoes for the band and win free VIP tickets, but the entry deadline was yesterday, and I only found out about it today." I sigh. "I just wish I could have entered, so at least I'd have a chance of going to the concert."

"That's too bad." Leila *tsk-tsk*s. "But have faith. You never know when your wish will come true."

"'If wishes were horses, beggars would ride,'" I say,

remembering the *Ye Olde Book of Nursery Rhymes* Granny Robicheaux used to read to me when I was little.

"'If turnips were watches, I'd wear one by my side,'" Leila says. "I read that book too."

She closes the one on her lap and puts it in a silver tote bag on the floor next to her.

"It's been great to meet you, Araminta," she says, getting up from her chair. "I'll see you around."

"See you," I say, wondering if she's a regular here at Starcups.

I look down at my shoe idea for Theo Downey, inspired by "You're My Only Dream Girl." It's not half bad, if I do say so myself. I'm starting to sketch an idea for lead guitarist Jimmy Strage when I see Leila passing the window. She waves, and I lift my hand in greeting. The bird on the parking meter flaps its wings and flies off in the same direction as Leila.

It's only after she's out of sight that it strikes me: I never told her my name.

"Where have you been?" Aunt Lottie asks the minute I walk through the door to the apartment. "We've been waiting to hear about your day!"

"Have you made lots of new little friends?" Aunt Margaux asks.

"A few," I admit. Livvy is really nice, and I guess I can count Eva as a new friend. She asked me to sit at her table at lunch and invited me over to her house tomorrow. "I'm hanging out with two of them after school tomorrow."

"See, we were right!" Aunt Lottie crows. "I knew filming the commercial there would help."

More like help drive me to the point of insanity from hearing the Youth rap so many times.

"So . . . how long ago did you arrange all this?" I ask.

"We'd already gotten a permit to film in New York City," Aunt Margaux explains. "But then Ella told us you were unhappy about the move."

"So we decided we'd switch the shoot location to your school," Aunt Lottie says. "At first Mr. Hamilton was reluctant to take the time away from 'educational pursuits,' but slipping him a big check for enrichment programs at the school took care of any lingering concerns."

I'm reminded that Principal Hamilton can be bought off with a big-enough donation. Sadly, I doubt the birthday money and allowance I have saved would be enough to satisfy his requirements.

❧

The aunties are all ready to walk me to school the next morning. There's no way I'm letting that happen again.

"Please tell me you're not filming another commercial," I groan.

"We know that it helped you," Aunt Lottie says. "You can't tell us it didn't."

I'm not going to admit anything if it means they're taking me to school.

"Aayesha says we've got enough material," Aunt Margaux says.

"Great. So I can walk to school by myself," I tell them. "Mom and Dad let me."

Aunt Lottie makes a tutting sound, with her hands on her hips. Aunt Margaux shakes her head.

"So irresponsible of them," she mutters.

"Look what happened to that young girl with the adorable matching red cap and cape when she went walking into the woods by herself," Aunt Lottie adds. She lowers her voice. "She ended up *inside a wolf.*"

"Yeah, okay. But she got out," I observe. "So did her grandmother."

"Only because a huntsman came along at the

right time," Aunt Lottie says. "You can't count on that happening."

"Not in Central Park, anyway," I say, trying to lighten the mood. "But don't worry, I'm not going there."

They aren't amused. My aunties have convinced themselves that I face imminent death if I walk out the front door alone.

"Please let me go by myself," I beg. "People sang your jingles at me in every single class yesterday."

"They did?" Aunt Margaux says, her face brightening. "That's wonderful! It means they're catchy!"

"Which one did they sing the most?" Aunt Lottie asks. "I want to know which ones are catching on with the youths. It's good feedback for the marketing department."

"I bet it was the Youth rap," Aunt Margaux says. "I wrote that one."

"Oh please, Marge!" Aunt Lottie says, raising a scornful eyebrow. "I'm sure it was 'If you think your life sucks'—in other words, *mine*."

"Ridiculous!" Aunt Margaux retorts. "And don't call me Marge. You know how much I hate that."

I'm pretty sure that's why Aunt Lottie does it, but

I decide to make my escape from the apartment while they're arguing. They're so busy shouting at each other that they don't even notice.

I walk to school enjoying the peace and quiet, which would sound crazy to anyone who lives in New York City—or any city, for that matter. But the hustle-and-bustle morning city noises are soothing after spending extended time with my aunts—at least until a police car starts its siren just as it passes by me, and I nearly jump out of my skin.

Chapter Five

"**NINA TELLS ME YOU'RE ONE OF EVA'S ELITES** now," Dakota says as soon as I sit next to him in social studies. From the tone of his voice, I sense he doesn't view this as a good thing.

"I . . . um . . . I think she was more impressed by my aunties than by me," I say, trying to downplay it. "And we both like Retro of Sync."

Dakota rolls his eyes. "Please don't tell me you're obsessed with Theo Downey too. Nina thinks he's 'soooooooooooooo dreamy.'"

He imitates his sister in a silly, high-pitched voice, which makes it clear he does not share my views on the complete adorableness of Retro of Sync's lead singer. That is fine. He's entitled to his opinion—even if it's totally wrong—but he shouldn't make fun of those of us who know that Theo is hunkalicious.

"Look, you haven't even been here for a full week yet," Dakota continues. "So let me give you a heads-up: Watch your back with Eva."

"What do you mean?" I ask him.

He pins me with his gaze. "Just be careful."

"So you're giving me all these mysterious dire warnings about Eva, but you won't tell me why?" I shrug. "It's not because you're jealous, right?"

His eyes widen with surprise and then narrow. "That's what you think? Wow. Okay. Suit yourself, Minty."

He turns away from me as if I've suddenly developed a really horrible smell.

It's like a slap in the face, and I'm hurt, but also mad. Just because Eva hasn't ever invited *him* to sit at her table, it doesn't mean *I* shouldn't be friendly with her.

Except it turns out it's not just Dakota warning me about my new sort-of friend. When I bump into Aria, Sophie, and Nina in the hallway between classes, Aria puts her hand on my arm and says, "Minty, we saw you sitting with Eva yesterday. Just . . . be careful."

"Yeah, Eva never does anything without an ulterior motive," Sophie adds.

What I don't want to tell them is that I have one too—to get my shoe designs to Theo Downey. So I decide to blame the fact that I'm glomming on to Eva and her "Elites" on my parents. Serves them right for uprooting me from my life and then leaving me.

"I'm so new at Manhattan World Themes," I say. "My parents told me I should get to know as many people as possible before committing to one particular friend group."

"I thought your parents were away," Sophie says, her brow furrowed.

"Uh . . . yeah. They said that before they left," I say.

"Well, don't say we didn't warn you," Aria says with a shrug.

"I won't," I say. "By the way, that skirt is adorable."

"I made it," she says. "My parents finally got over their aichmophobia enough to let me get a sewing machine."

"Ache-moe-what?" I ask.

"Aichmophobia. It's a fear of sharp objects. My parents didn't want me around any because of, ya know, that whole *prick your finger and fall asleep for one hundred years* thing," Aria says.

"Oh yeah. I saw the episode of *Teen Couture* where you confronted that guy about trying to kill you," I say. "What was his name?"

"Jesse," Aria says. "He's the grandson of the woman who put the curse on Mom."

"That was totally cray," I say.

"Cray is an understatement," Sophie says. "And that was only what you saw on TV. There was so much more behind the scenes."

"Yeah, stealing the Devil's Dipstick from the Brooklyn Botanic Garden was . . ." Nina trails off, a faraway look in her eyes. "I thought I was going to faint."

"You're not the only one who thought you were going to faint," Sophie mutters.

Just then I hear someone shout, "*Minty*—I need to talk to you!" from down the hall behind me. I turn around and it's Eva, with a disgruntled expression on her face.

"Uh, sorry, got to go," I tell the other girls. As I turn back to Eva, I catch Sophie rolling her eyes. Whatever. I really like Aria, Nina, and Sophie, but it's not like I have to stay glued to them all the time, right?

When I walk over to Eva, she immediately grabs me by the arm and leans her head close to mine. "What are you doing talking to *them*?" she asks. "It won't help you be a social success at MWTMS."

"But they're—"

"Nobodies," Eva says. "Trust me."

"Aria was on *Teen Couture*," I say, feeling a need to defend my other new friend's somebodyhood. "And—"

"Do you want to be in the top tier here or don't you?" Eva says, glaring at me through narrowed eyes.

At my old school, I didn't even have to think about whether I was "top tier" or not. I guess when your grand-parents are the king and queen, you're considered the cream of the social crop just by accident of birth. It's strange to suddenly be expected to work for it when it's something you've always taken for granted.

Another reason to be mad at my parents for moving me here.

"Yes," I say. "I do."

"So stop hanging out with losers," Eva says.

They're so not losers, but Eva is the one with con-nections that might help me get to see Retro of Sync. I nod, so she assumes I agree with her, and try my best to ignore the little voice inside that tells me I'm acting a little too much like Horrible Hortensia for comfort.

"I'll meet you and Livvy out front after school," Eva

says cheerfully. "I had our housekeeper make chocolate chip cookies."

"See you then," I say, but as I go into my next class, I think about how the best part of having cookies when hanging out with friends is making them ourselves. I guess maybe things are different when you're crazy rich in New York City.

Livvy and I walk with Eva back to her duplex on Park Avenue. The lobby of her building screams, *People with lots and lots of money live here*. The doorman is wearing an ornate uniform that wouldn't look out of place on the soldiers guarding Buckingham Palace. When the elevator stops at Eva's floor, it really *is* her floor: The Murgatroyd apartment is the only one there.

Eva lets herself in the door, and a woman in a gray uniform with a crisp white apron greets us as soon as we walk in.

"Good afternoon, Miss Eva. Did you have a good day at school?"

"Yeah. Did you make the cookies?"

"Yes, Miss Eva. Do you want them in the dining room?"

"No, bring them to my room with three glasses of milk," Eva tells her. Then, turning to us, she says, "Come on, let's go to my bedroom. We have lots to discuss."

My grandparents on Dad's side live in a literal castle, but there's more opulent gold going on in just the first few rooms of Eva's apartment than there is in all of Chateau de Robicheaux.

"Do you ever get used to coming here?" I whisper to Livvy as Eva leads the way to her room.

"We live in a two-bedroom walk-up," Livvy whispers back as we follow Eva down a hallway lined with photographs of her parents with famous people. "That would be a firm no."

Eva's room, which is four times the size of mine, has a large canopy bed with pink and gold swags. Despite its grandeur, the room would send my mom into a conniption because there are clothes and shoes strewn *everywhere*. I didn't think anyone our age could *own* so many clothes. It looks like Eva emptied out all her closets (I count three) onto the floor before school this morning.

There are also posters and pictures of Theo Downey tacked onto every possible surface. The room is a shrine to both Theo and being a total slob.

"Wow. I thought I was a Theo Downey fangirl, but you've got me beat," I say, trying not to be too obvious about my gawking.

"Oh please, Minty. I am Theo's number one fan," Eva declares. "No one else even comes close."

She puts on a Retro of Sync playlist, and starts dancing to "I Heard She Loves You."

"Can we go to the kitchen and get the cookies?" Livvy asks. "I need food."

"Relax. Marta is bringing them," Eva says.

"When?" Livvy asks. "I'm starving."

Eva huffs and goes to the door. "MARTA!" she shouts. "CAN WE GET THOSE COOKIES ALREADY? AND DON'T FORGET THE MILK!"

Then she comes back, turns down the music slightly, and lounges on one of the four big beanbag chairs in the room, which look like fluffy gold and pink islands emerging from the waves of crumpled clothing.

"Make yourselves comfortable," she says, waving an arm at the other beanbags.

Livvy takes a pink one, and I lower myself into a gold one after removing three sweaters and a pair of jeans from it and placing them on the floor with the rest of the clothing debris.

"So, I've come up with a plan," Eva announces. "The. Best. Plan. Ever."

"Best plan ever for what?" I ask.

"Duh! For meeting Theo Downey, of course!" Eva says. "And getting your shoe designs to him, even though it's past the competition deadline."

Livvy rolls her eyes. "So what's plan number . . . what is it, twenty zillion and two?"

Eva gives her a quelling look. "It doesn't matter—all the previous plans were practice runs for the complete, foolproof perfection of this one."

"Okay, lay it on us," Livvy says. "I can't *wait* to hear the latest—"

"Well, my dad found out from a business colleague who learned from a hotelier he plays squash with at the Harvard Club that Retro of Sync is going to be staying at Hotel Z in midtown, because it's not too far from Madison Square Garden," Eva says. "Now that we know where they're staying, it makes it easier to meet Theo."

"Won't the security be pretty tight?" I ask.

"Oh yeah," Livvy says. "When Quicksilver Crossroads stayed at the Plaza, fans had to stand behind barriers, and they had security at every door so it was impossible to sneak in."

"That won't be a problem for *us*," Eva says, her nose in the air. "Because we're going to already be inside the hotel."

Livvy and I exchange a glance.

"How?" I ask. "I'm pretty sure we're too young to rent a room."

"Not to mention too broke," Livvy adds.

"That's an amateur move," Eva says, like she's got a degree in lead-singer stalking. "It's *so* obvious."

"Fine, Miss Expert," Livvy says. "What's your latest, greatest idea?"

"Well, when Daddy told me he knew where they were staying, I said I wanted to get an internship at that hotel, because I'm too young to get a job, but it's so important to get work experience and blah blah blah, all that boring stuff I knew he'd totally want to hear," Eva says. "He said he'd speak to the hotel owner. And the hotel owner said yes!" Looking at us triumphantly, she says, "We start on Thursday after school, which happens to be the day that Retro of Sync checks in before kicking off their world tour on Saturday."

Mom always says if something sounds too good to be true, it is too good to be true—well, except for my dad, who she claims lived up to his billing.

Eva's plan definitely sounds too good to be true.

"It must be so nice to have relatives with connections in high places," Livvy says. I don't blame her for sounding a little snarky.

"You don't have to be jealous, Livvy," Eva says. "Because last night I told Dad that my two underprivileged friends need internships too."

I glance over at Livvy to see if she's having the same reaction I am to that. She's busy glaring at Eva.

"What do you mean, 'underprivileged friends'?" she says, doing air quotes with her fingers.

"My grandparents live in a literal castle back home," I point out.

"I meant it relatively. Like compared to me," Eva says to Livvy. Then she turns to me. "Minty, your grandparents might be royalty, but your mom started her life as a glorified maid."

Wow. I might be mad at my parents for moving me here and taking off to Europe, but no one gets to talk about my mom that way. *I'm* the only one who is allowed to do that.

"My mom might have started life as a glorified maid, but she's built a really successful cleaning-products company," I say. "Which is embarking on a global expansion as we speak."

"And just because my parents aren't gazillionaires it doesn't mean we're poor," Livvy says, sounding distinctly miffed.

"Will you two relax? There's nothing the matter with being poor," Eva says.

"Tell that to people who don't have enough money for rent, clothes, and groceries," Livvy says.

"Omigod, can you stop getting so hung up on the fact I called you underprivileged friends?" Eva snaps. "I only told him that because then the hotel could feel like it's doing a corporate good deed. Otherwise, they might not let all three of us be interns."

That kind of makes sense in a roundabout way, but I'm still not willing to let Eva off the hook that easily, because . . . well, because what she said was rude and insulting.

I glance over at Livvy, who opens her mouth to say something, but then there's a knock on the door, and Marta comes in bearing a tray with a plate of delicious-smelling cookies and three glasses of milk. There's even a little white rose in a small silver vase. It's like getting room service in a fancy hotel—until Marta trips over a pair of boots half buried by a cashmere sweater, and milk and cookies go flying everywhere as she releases the tray to break her fall.

I end up with a few cookies in my lap and milk splatter in my hair. Livvy gets some milk splatter on her clothes, but the bulk of the spray ends up on Eva. She is not happy, which she lets us know by emitting an ear-piercing shriek.

"Marta! Look at my shirt! Do you know how much this cost?" she yells.

"Stain Slayer will get it out," I say without thinking.

I've gone over to the dark side. I sound like one of Mom's commercials.

"I'm so sorry, Miss Eva!" Marta says, lifting herself off the floor slowly and what looks like painfully. She rubs one of her wrists. I can't understand why she's apologizing to Eva and not the other way around. How can Eva blame Marta for tripping over the debris in her room? Besides, if she cares so much about her expensive clothes, why are they scattered all over the place instead of hanging neatly in her closet?

Help! I'm turning into my mother.

"Are you okay?" I ask Marta. "Should I get you some ice for your wrist?"

She seems surprised by my question.

"Marta, we need towels and more cookies," Eva says.

"I'll get them now, Miss Eva," Marta says, picking up the tray, the cookies, and the glasses, which didn't shatter because the piles of clothing provided a soft landing.

As soon as she leaves the room, Livvy turns to Eva. "Did you have to be so mean to Marta? She wouldn't have tripped if your floor wasn't such a messy minefield."

"She's the *housekeeper*. My parents *pay* her to clean up," Eva says as she gets out of the beanbag and goes to one of her three closets. "If I cleaned up after myself, Marta wouldn't have a job. Now do you want me to lend you some clothes so you don't have to hang out with milk and cookie crumbs all over, or don't you?"

She throws open the closet door to reveal a walk-in that's almost as big as my bedroom. Turning to look at us, she says, "Well? What are you waiting for?"

I've only got a little milk on my shirt, but if Eva's willing to let me into her wardrobe wonderland, I'm not about to say no.

Livvy and I follow her into the closet, which has a life-size poster of Theo Downey on the door.

"Are all three of your closets this size?" I ask.

"This is the biggest," Eva says.

"But the other ones are almost as big," Livvy tells me.

I can't believe someone my age has so much clothing.

Don't Eva's parents ever say, *We're not going to buy you too many clothes because you're just going to grow out of them in six months*? Mine do. Constantly. I can't wait to stop growing so they don't have the excuse anymore. I just hope I get a few inches taller before that happens.

She pulls a turquoise shirt off a hanger and hands it to me. "This would look good on you, Minty."

The fabric is so luxurious and soft that I can't help but look at the label. It's one that I recognize from *Haute Couture* magazine.

"Are you sure?" I ask. "This shirt must have cost a fortune. What if I get something on it?"

"Don't worry," Eva says breezily. "I'm sure your mother has some miraculous cleaning product that will get it off."

She hands Livvy an adorable long-sleeve T-shirt with GIRL POWER! on it and finds a cashmere sweater for herself.

"Come on, let's change," Eva says, walking out of the closet.

As much as I love Theo Downey, I'm a little weirded out by the fact that he's staring at me from all directions.

"Doesn't it freak you out to get undressed with Theo watching you?" I ask.

Eva looks at me like I'm a complete simpleton. "You realize they're just *posters*, right?"

"Of course I do!" I say. "But there are so many of them it feels like we're being watched."

"I know, right?" Livvy says. "I had a hard time falling asleep when I slept over that time, because I was convinced Theo's eyes were following me."

I turn toward the wall with the fewest Theos and change into Eva's shirt. The material is so soft I feel wealthier just wearing it.

Marta comes back with more milk and cookies. She waits at the door like she's afraid to enter and risk her health and Eva's wrath again. Livvy goes to take the tray from her.

"Thanks, Marta," Livvy says.

"How is your wrist?" I ask.

"I'm going to ice it now," Marta says, heading back to the kitchen.

I clear a patch of floor between the beanbag chairs so Livvy has somewhere to put down the tray.

"Less than forty-eight hours till we get to see Theo up close and personal," Eva says, her eyes dreamy. "I don't know how I'm going to sleep between now and then."

"How long does this internship last?" Livvy asks.

"And will they write us a recommendation if we do a good job?"

Eva gives her a pitying look. "Oh, honey, you don't think we're actually going to *work*, do you?"

"Isn't that kind of the point of having an internship?" I ask.

"Not this one," Eva says. "The only point of this one is to get us inside the Hotel Z. As soon as we meet Theo, it's *hasta la vista* internship."

That sounds all kinds of wrong to me. But I'm not about to speak up, because I want to go to the concert more than anything, and Eva's plan is my only chance.

Instead I grab one of the chocolate chip cookies Marta brought. It melts in my mouth in a delicious swirl of chocolate and cookie.

"You guys have got to see the latest pics of Theo," Eva says. She shows us some seriously adorable photos that have been posted to TheoDowneyIsaDreamboat.com, one of the many fan sites for Retro of Sync's lead singer.

I think he's cute and super talented, but I've got homework to do, so I can't spend the entire afternoon hanging around looking at pictures of Theo. I make it obvious that I'm checking the time on my phone.

"Omigod! I better get home before the aunties call

911 to report me missing!" I exclaim, mentally apologizing to Lottie and Margaux for using them as an excuse for leaving.

"Yeah, me too," Livvy says. "Well, the needing-to-get-home part. Not the aunties-calling-911 part."

"Say hi to your aunties for me," Eva tells me. "Ask them if I can be in another commercial."

I just smile uneasily. The last thing I want to do is encourage further communication between the aunties and anyone at MWTMS. Between Aunt Lottie and Aunt Margaux bribing (sorry, I mean giving a big donation to) my principal and people quoting my family's commercials at me constantly, how will I ever be able to be my own person?

"See you tomorrow," I say, without promising Eva anything. "Should we take the tray back to the kitchen on our way out?"

"No, don't worry. Marta will get it," Eva says.

Livvy and I show ourselves out. We ride down in the elevator without saying a word. But as soon as we get halfway down the block, she says, "Is it just me, or do you have a bad feeling about Eva's plan too?"

"No, it's not just you."

"Eva's my friend, but sometimes when she decides

she's got a great idea . . . well, there's no talking her out of it," Livvy says with a sigh.

"So . . . do you think we should back out?" I ask, hoping she says no, because going along with Eva's plan is the only chance I have to win tickets to the ROS concert.

"Possibly," Livvy says. "But Eva won't take it well. Trust me. She won't."

I believe Livvy. I'm afraid of what Eva will do if that's the choice I make. Livvy's been her friend for years, so eventually she'll be forgiven. I've only been her sort-of friend since yesterday. But even though I'm not 100 percent sure Eva's plan will work, I don't want to give up on it while there's the slightest hope I can get my designs in front of Theo Downey.

It's times like this I wish Mom and Dad weren't so busy jet-setting off to Europe to make big deals, because I actually want to *ask* their advice instead of them giving it unsolicited like they usually do. Since they're away, I'm going to have to ask my aunties, since they are in loco parentis.

When I get home, it's apparent that the aunties have been attempting to cook something for dinner, because the smoke alarm is going off and Aunt Lottie is on the phone with the fire department.

"I'm telling you, it's okay! You don't have to come! The fire is already out," she shouts into the phone. "I don't care if you already sent out the fire engine—call it back!"

Aunt Margaux is standing by the sink in a smoky haze, trying to scrape carbonized black lumps—which look like once upon a time they might have been lamb chops—out of a blackened frying pan. Her hair is frizzed around her angular face, and she has a big smudge of soot across her forehead.

"Well *helloooooooo*, CinderAuntie!" I say.

"Not funny," she says, scowling. "I *can* cook, you know."

I look from her face to the frying pan and back. "I totally believe you, Aunt Margaux. It's just . . ." I think of a lie that will spare both her feelings and my stomach. "It's just that well-done meat gives me indigestion."

She drops the pan into the sink and sighs.

"Me too," she admits. "I can run a successful multimillion-dollar company, but whenever I cook, things tend to catch fire."

"Maybe that's 'cause you always left the cooking to Mom," I say. "But I bet you can learn if you put your mind to it."

Aunt Margaux nods slowly. "Good thinking, Minty,"

she says. "Our mother would have rather died than set foot in the kitchen. But I'm sick of ordering out all the time. I want to be able to cook. And bake. Especially bake."

"When the kitchen recovers, I can teach you how to make cookies," I say.

"Oatmeal raisin? Like Ella used to make?" Aunt Margaux says, her face transforming from glum to hopeful.

"Yeah. Mom taught me how to make those. Chocolate chip cookies too."

"Yes!" she says, pumping her fist. "Hey, Lottie, you done with the fire department? We need to order some dinner."

Aunt Lottie comes in, phone in hand. "How about Chinese?" she says.

"Sounds good to me," I say.

"Minty's going to teach me how to make Ella's oatmeal raisin cookies," Aunt Margaux says.

"Not tonight," Aunt Lottie says. "I've argued with the fire department enough for one day. The smoke still hasn't cleared from your latest cooking attempt."

"Of course not tonight," Aunt Margaux says, folding her arms across her chest. "Tomorrow or the next day."

Aunt Lottie rolls her eyes and looks up the menu for Hunan Gourmet Balcony on her phone. We order the food, and I decide now's as good a time as any to ask the aunties for their advice.

"This is a purely hypothetical question," I say. "But let's say someone, maybe a friend, is doing something kind of over-the-top to get the attention of a guy that she likes . . . Would you have any advice for that friend?"

My aunts look at each other and burst out laughing. I'm talking serious guffaws. Aunt Margaux wipes her eyes on her sleeve, she's laughing so hard.

"You're asking *us* that question?" Aunt Lottie gasps finally.

"Uh . . . yeah," I say.

"I cut off my own left toes to try to convince Robbie that the shoe fit and I was his true love," Aunt Margaux says, like anyone could ever forget something that gross about a relative.

"And I cut off my left heel!" Aunt Lottie says, with what seems like an unnatural amount of hilarity in her voice. "How much more over-the-top can you get?"

They sound proud of the extremes they went to in order to one-up each other in cheating so that they could marry Dad, like it was the Hunger Games of the marriage mart. Come to think of it, it kind of was.

It makes me glad I'm an only child and my parents won't ever do something like that. At least I hope they won't. . . .

"This isn't *that* over-the-top," I say. "No self-mutilation is involved."

"Good," Aunt Lottie says. "I wouldn't want to have to explain missing toes to Ella and Robbie."

"Does our little Minty have a crushy-wushy?" Margaux says in a baby-talk voice.

Barf! I should have known that asking the aunties would be a mistake.

"No!" I exclaim. "It really is a friend!" Then I realize my blunder. "I mean, hypothetically speaking."

The aunties exchange a glance.

"So what exactly is this hypothetical friend planning to do in order to get the guy's attention?" Aunt Lottie asks, doing air quotes with her fingers when she says "hypothetical friend."

"Is it anything that would get this friend hurt or arrested?" Aunt Margaux asks.

"Or anyone else hurt or arrested?" Aunt Lottie adds.

"No. She got her dad to get her an internship where the guy is stay—going to be," I say, trying to be as vague as possible. "But as soon as she gets to meet him, she's going to ditch the internship."

Aunt Lottie gasps and claps her hand over her heart. Aunt Margaux shakes her head disapprovingly.

"That's a very bad idea," she says. "It wouldn't be good for her future in the workplace. Your hypothetical friend would look flighty and irresponsible."

That's not good. It might not matter to Eva, but it would matter to me. I might be the granddaughter of the king and queen of Robicheaux, but my parents expect me to work as hard as they do. And, as Mom is always so fond of telling me, that's *very* hard.

"I'm glad you're not the one who is hypothetically doing it," Aunt Margaux says. "I don't want to have to call Ella and Robbie while they're in Europe to say you're in trouble, hypothetically or not. Not after she finally trusts us to look after you."

I stare at her. "You mean Mom didn't trust you before?"

Aunt Lottie laughs. "Would you? She only asked us because your grandmother was busy planning another ball and she was desperate."

"Can you blame her?" Margaux says. "We tormented the poor girl!"

"Remember when we took her bed away and made her sleep by the fireplace?" Aunt Lottie says with a giggle.

"How could I forget? That's why we started calling her Cinderella!" Aunt Margaux says. "Well, that and throwing the lentils and peas into the ashes and making her pick them out."

My aunts seem to be enjoying these cruel memories a little too much for comfort. I wonder again what possessed my parents to leave them in charge of their darling daughter.

"So that's why when I tried being vegetarian for a week, Mom refused to make anything that had peas or lentils in it," I say. "It's all *your* fault!"

"Guilty as charged," Aunt Lottie says, with what sounds alarmingly like pride. "But look at what our bullying did for your mom. . . . If it weren't for us making her into our Cinderwench, she wouldn't have been inspired to create the Crud Crusher and the Dust Decimator and the Stain Slayer. It's like we're responsible for the House of Robicheaux cleaning empire."

"Which is now expanding globally, hence why we're

here looking after you," Aunt Margaux points out.

"Thanks to us, your mother developed *grit*!" Aunt Lottie says. "You could almost say Ella owes her success to us."

Almost.

I just hope they're not planning a grit-development program for me.

"So other than not cutting off any body parts, and that this is possibly jeopardizing her future in the workplace, do you have any more advice for my friend? Hypothetically, I mean."

The aunties exchange a glance. Aunt Lottie nods.

"All's fair in love and war," Aunt Margaux says. "That's what Mother always told us."

As I head to my room to work on my homework and, more important, the sketches for the contest, I realize that the only thing that conversation did was confuse me even more. Maybe that's a good thing. If I want to try to get my designs in front of Theo Downey, I can't let anyone be talked out of it—most of all myself.

Chapter Six

DAKOTA IS STILL KIND OF FROSTY IN SOCIAL
studies the next morning. He barely says hi when I slide
into the desk next to him. I've been thinking about what
Aria and Nina said about how I should join Couture
Club, so I ask him when the next meeting is—even
though I already know—as a way of breaking the ice.

"It's after school today," he says, without looking
at me.

"Great. I'm going to give it a try."

That gets his full attention.

"Are you sure? You won't find any of 'Eva's Elites'
there. It's not their kind of club."

I stare at him. "Do you really think that matters to me?"

His gaze drops down to his boots. "I don't know." Then he looks up, fixing me with his brown eyes, and asks: "Does it?"

"No," I tell him, hurt that he would think it would. "Just because I sit with Eva at lunch, it doesn't mean she controls my life."

"That's what you think," he says. "You must not have read the Eva's Elites handbook yet."

I remember Eva saying I shouldn't hang out with Sophie, Aria, and Nina because they're losers, and I wonder if there really *is* an Eva's Elites handbook. That would be way too weird. Still, as much as I need Eva to get my designs to Retro of Sync, I'm not about to let her be the boss of me.

"Actually, what I think is that I'll see you at the meeting after school."

"Welcome back from the dark side," he says, breaking into a huge grin as he pushes the wool beanie he always wears back on his thick, dark hair. "It's good to have you back."

"I didn't realize I'd ever left," I say.

He laughs.

"But I'm looking forward to Couture Club," I add.

And I am, especially when Dakota tells me he'll meet me after school so we can go together. "That way I can introduce you to Ms. Amara."

I'm so excited about that, I make the mistake of telling Livvy about it at lunch within earshot of Eva.

"Why would you want to hang out with the dorks at Couture Club?" she says. "They only pretend to be couture because they can't afford the real thing."

"*Couture* means 'dressmaking' in French," I point out, a fact I only know because Granny Robicheaux told me. "So they aren't pretending at all."

"I meant couture like clothes designed and made by famous designers," Eva says airily. "Not sew-your-own-clothes. But if you want to waste your time at Couture Club, that's your decision." She narrows her eyes. "As long as you don't forget we have our *internship* tomorrow."

"How could I forget?" I say.

"Good," she says. "It's going to be so much more awesome than Couture Club."

If I end up getting my designs to Theo Downey, she might be right.

❧

Dakota meets me outside my last-period class. As we walk to Ms. Amara's classroom, we find out that we've got more in common than social studies and a love of designing things—like New York City pizza, for example.

"If you think Giovanni's pizza is good, we should go to Mario's. Theirs is even better," Dakota tells me.

"I'm up for that," I say, wondering if he means that we should go in a date way or a friends-who-like-pizza way. Then he stops and turns to me, a flush slowly rising from the collar of his plaid flannel shirt.

"Maybe we could go after Couture Club," he says.

I smile up at him. "Sure. I'd like that."

"Sounds like a plan," he says.

When we get to the room, Dakota introduces me to Ms. Amara.

"Welcome to Couture Club, Minty," she says warmly.

"I'm excited to be here," I tell her.

"Do you have a specific area of interest?" Ms. Amara asks me.

"Shoes," I tell her.

"Well, that makes sense," she says. I'm not sure if she means because of who my mom is or because of the aunties.

Taking out my sketchbook, I show her some of my latest designs.

"These are great!" she says. "I like this pair especially."

She points to the sketch of the sneakers I designed for Theo Downey to wear at the opening-night concert— the ones I'm hoping will win me tickets for the show if Eva's plan works tomorrow.

Aria and Nina walk into the classroom. Aria does a double take when she sees me talking to Ms. Amara.

"Oh . . . hi," she says. "I didn't expect to see you here."

"Why is that?" I ask.

"I don't know. You didn't seem that into the idea when I suggested it last week."

"Oh . . . well, I guess that was because I didn't want anyone to find out that I was related to the Comfortably Ever After ladies."

My admission is greeted with hilarity from the assembled members of the Manhattan World Themes Middle School Couture Club.

"Guess that whole *filming a commercial at our school* gave your secret away," Dakota says, his voice full of amusement.

"Yeah, it kind of did," I say. "In a very embarrassing way."

"I can see why it might have felt mortifying for you, Minty, but it was a great learning experience for our Couture Club members," Ms. Amara says, smiling. "They got to see firsthand all the work that goes into creating and shooting a commercial."

She walks around her desk and leans against the front of it.

"Let's talk about commercials for a moment," she says. "What works and what doesn't?"

"Let me guess—the aunties' ads don't work," I say. "They are *so* cringeworthy."

Ms. Amara laughs. "How many of you can tell me the words of a Comfortably Ever After spot?"

There's a cacophony of sounds as every single person in the room besides Ms. Amara and me starts rapping the words to various ads for the aunties' shoes. I don't know why I'm surprised. Kids have been reciting them to me ever since they realized I was related to the aunties by my grandfather's marriage to their mother.

"That's a measure of a successful ad—when people remember it," Ms. Amara says. "It's known as a 'recall test.'"

I make a mental note to tell the aunties this good news—except that will probably cause an argument over which aunt's ideas had better recall . . . yeah, on second thought, I'll keep it to myself.

The project of the day is to design an accessory. It's a no-brainer for me to choose shoes, because I'm obsessing about my designs for the contest. I experiment with the look I created for the Retro of Sync bassist, Chad Apollo, based on their song "Rock-'n'-Roll Planet." They're thick-soled sneakers with a cosmos background on the canvas uppers. A bass travels through, trailed by a comet's plume of musical notes.

"You've really got a talent for shoe design," Ms. Amara says as she looks over my shoulder. "It must be in the family."

Like they say, if the shoe fits . . .

The end of the session comes as a surprise because I've been enjoying myself so much.

"I hope you'll come back," Ms. Amara tells me when I say good-bye.

I promise that I will.

"So, are we heading to Mario's?" Dakota asks me.

"Oh yes," Nina says. "I could really go for a slice."

"Me too," Aria says. "I'm starving!"

"Uh . . . ," Dakota says, giving Nina a pointed look.

"What?" she asks.

"Um . . . nothing," he says, brushing a nonexistent piece of lint off his coat with studied nonchalance.

"I give you my brother, Dakota—a man of few words," Nina says.

Dakota shoots her a dirty look, which she blithely ignores.

As we walk the few blocks to Mario's, we stop and critique the fashions in different store windows. Aria likes more colorful pieces than Nina, who prefers earth tones. Dakota is a minimalist with a thing for camo.

There's a shoe store with a small selection of Comfortably Ever After™ shoes—some of the aunties' more flamboyant designs.

"Can we skip this one?" I ask.

"Oh, come on, this was going to be the most fun!" Aria says.

"I thought you were starving," Dakota says. "If we do every single window, we'll never make it to Mario's."

"Okay, fine," Aria says. "Take all my fun away."

I smile at Dakota and mouth, *Thanks.*

Mario's is a hole-in-the-wall place in a ritzy area. You'd barely notice it among the stores selling high fashion, expensive leather goods, and art. But the pizza . . .

"Omigod," I say. "This is crazy delish."

"Told you," Dakota says with a grin. He's got a small blob of tomato sauce on his cheek.

"Bro, wipe your face," Nina says. Then, turning to Aria and me, she says, "Can't take him anywhere."

Aria starts telling us some funny stories about her time on *Teen Couture* when Dakota gets up to go to the bathroom.

As soon as he's out of earshot, Nina and Aria exchange a glance.

"I think Dakota likes you," Nina says.

"What makes you say that?" I ask, hoping she's right.

"Because he's been looking at you every other second," she says. "And he laughs more when you're around."

I feel a glow inside, and it's not because I just ate some warm, gooey cheese.

But then I wonder if that's weird for Nina.

"Would it bother you if . . . well, if I liked him back?"

She shrugs. "Not really." Then she smiles. "My condition for being okay with it is you get him to dress better. I'm serious—the guy has more plaid flannel shirts than any human should be allowed to own."

"Maybe to him flannel shirts are like shoes are to me," I say. "Like, there's no such thing as too many."

Nina gives me a pained look. "Please don't encourage him."

"I can't promise to get him to dress better, but I can promise not to encourage him to buy any more flannel shirts," I say.

Aria giggles. "That sounds fair," she says, just as Dakota comes back to the table.

"What sounds fair?" he asks.

Aria, Nina, and I look at one another and we all explode laughing. My sides start hurting because I can't stop.

"Why do I get the impression you guys were talking smack about me?" he says. "That's the only thing Nina would find this funny."

That just makes us all laugh harder.

When I've finally stopped enough to be able to breathe, I check the time. "I better get back before the aunties start worrying," I say. "They're afraid I'll be eaten by wolves."

"Uh . . . that would be a lot more likely where we used to live in Canada than in New York City," Dakota says.

"I know, right?" I say. "But try telling that to Margaux and Lottie."

I tell them I'll see them all tomorrow, and wave good-bye.

❧

The aunties are in the living room when I get home. Aunt Lottie is flipping through some of Mom's cookbooks. Aunt Margaux is on her laptop, and she must be really involved in whatever she's doing because she doesn't even look up when I go in and tell them I'm home.

"How was your day?" Aunt Lottie asks.

"Good. I had fun at Couture Club and then had pizza."

"Obviously too busy to teach me how to make Ella's oatmeal raisin cookies," Aunt Margaux says.

She might be a grown-up and head of a multimillion-dollar shoe empire, but Aunt Margaux is putting on a kid-worthy sulk right about now.

"Warn me when it happens, Minty," Aunt Lottie says. "So I can tell the fire department to be on high alert."

If looks could kill, Lottie would be a goner and Aunt Margaux would be under arrest for sororicide.

I feel bad. I didn't realize my aunt thought I was definitely going to teach her how to make cookies this afternoon. Margaux seems like such a tough nut, but apparently there's a soft core encased in that hard shell.

"I'm so sorry, Aunt Margaux," I say. "Dakota suggested going to Mario's after Couture Club, and I just—"

"Ooh! Who is this Dakota?" Aunt Lottie asks, and I curse myself for having let his name slip.

"He's just a guy in my social studies class," I say in what I hope is a totally nonchalant manner.

Unfortunately, the sudden flush of my cheeks gives me away.

"Margaux! Minty's got a crush!" Aunt Lottie says, clapping her hands with excitement.

"So she forgets her promise to teach her boring old aunt how to make cookies," Aunt Margaux says, her eyes fixed on her laptop.

"I really am sorry," I tell her. "How about tomorrow? I have . . . uh, something right after school, but when I get home."

That finally cracks Margaux's ice. "Promise?"

"Promise," I say, and her mouth thaws into a smile.

I head to my room to work on my homework. I'm up late into the night preparing the drawings of my designs for the Retro of Sync competition. I just hope it's not too late.

Chapter Seven

TODAY IS THEO DAY. EVEN IF I WANTED TO
forget that fact, Eva texted Livvy and me at six thirty in
the morning saying: It's T minus 9!

I get out of bed with a growing sense of foreboding.
I had a hard time getting to sleep last night. Instead of
counting sheep, I was mentally listing all the ways Eva's
plan could go wrong.

After throwing on a cute skirt and the most interny
shirt I can find in my closet, I decide to wear my vintage
Trudy Neal ballet flats, because they always brighten up
my day.

Then I say good-bye to the aunties, who tell me they

are eating oatmeal because it "keeps them regular," whatever that means.

"Don't forget, you promised to teach me how to make Ella's oatmeal raisin cookies this afternoon," Aunt Margaux says, her face lit up with excitement.

Ugh. I had forgotten.

"When I get home. Yeah. But not right after school."

"Don't worry, Minty, I've already put the fire department on speed dial," Aunt Lottie says.

Aunt Margaux throws a piece of toast at Aunt Lottie, and I decide it's time to leave before there's a full-fledged food fight.

"See you later!" I call to them as I head out the door. "Try not to kill each other or burn the place down while I'm gone!"

They're too busy arguing to hear me.

Dakota and Nina walk into school at the same time I do. Dakota whispers something to Nina, and she waves and says hi, then heads off down the hallway.

"Hey, Minty, how's it going?" he asks.

"Okay, I guess," I say.

"That's not so convincing," he says.

"I'm just tired." I don't tell him it's because I was up

so late working on my contest entries, and that I'm really nervous about T Day.

Dakota shifts from one foot to the other. "I was thinking . . . do you maybe want to go to Starcups with me this afternoon?"

I do. I really do. But I also really want to go see Retro of Sync.

"I . . . can't. I'm doing something else," I tell him. His smile fades. "But I'd love to go another time."

"Cool," he says. "Let me know when you're up for it."

I wonder if I should tell Eva that I've had second thoughts (not to mention third, fourth, and fifth ones) about her plan, but I don't want to risk it. That would mean giving up any chance of going to see Retro of Sync. Why couldn't I have learned about the contest a day earlier?

My phone is buzzing in my pocket. "I just have to check my texts," I tell Dakota. "My phone is blowing up about something."

"No problem. I'll see you in social studies." He waves and heads toward our classroom.

Livvy: BE WARNED. I just told Eva I'm not going to do it.

Livvy: I said I was tired of taking the fall for her, and this plan is her worst idea yet.

Livvy: Spoiler alert: She didn't take it well.

Livvy: Called me a wimp, the world's worst BFF, etc. etc.

Livvy: Then she said: "Minty better not back out."

Livvy: She's looking for you right this very minute.

Livvy: Oh, and I'm no longer one of Eva's Elites, effective immediately. I have been ordered to sit elsewhere at lunch.

"Minty! There you are. I've been looking all over for you."

Eva is bearing down on me, looking determined.

"Well, here I am," I say with a weak smile.

"You won't believe this—Livvy chickened out on us."

I pretend this is news to me. "Really? Why?"

"She's a wimp, that's why. But you aren't, are you, Minty?"

"Wimp? Me? No way!" I declare, even though my stomach is giving me very wimpy signals as the words come out of my mouth. *Eyes on the prize!* I tell myself, imagining how I will show Theo Downey my designs and he'll love them so much he gives me a backstage pass to *all* the Retro of Sync concerts in New York City.

Eva links her arm in mine and starts walking with me down the hallway. "I knew I could count on you, Minty. You've got your aunts' blood in your veins."

I decide not to point out that they're my step-aunties, so technically I don't, because Eva's on a roll.

"You and me—we're a great team," she continues. "And in eight hours' time, we're going to meet Theo Downey, and Livvy will be kicking herself for not coming."

I hope she's right. Really, I do. But I can't help wondering if Livvy is the smart one and I'm about to make a big mistake.

At the end of each period, Eva texts me the latest countdown to T time. With each text, I get more nervous. I barely have an appetite by the time I get to lunch, because I'm so worried about everything that might go wrong.

When I get to the Eva's Elites table, Eva's busy telling Connor how he's not just going to owe her one cookie, he's going to owe her an entire box, because today is the day she's going to prove him wrong.

"How?" he asks.

"That's classified," she says.

"I'll believe it when I see it," Connor says. "But there better be more proof than that he liked one of your Pinstagrams."

"Oh, there will be," Eva says.

"Are you sure you should be telling people?" I whisper to Eva. "Isn't it better to keep this all under wraps until afterward?"

"It's not like I've told anyone the actual plan," she says.

"I know," I say. "You haven't even told *me* everything, and I'm supposed to be part of it."

"Don't worry so much, Minty. It'll give you wrinkles," Eva tells me, waving a dismissive hand a little too close to my nose for comfort. "I've got it all under control."

For some reason, I don't find that reassuring.

After school, I meet Eva and we take the bus down to midtown, where the Hotel Z is located. I've got my ROS-inspired shoe designs in an envelope, which I've tucked under my shirt because I'm pretty sure interns aren't allowed to carry backpacks around while they work. There's already a crowd of Retro of Sync fans standing behind police barriers to the right and left of the hotel entrance, and a policeman on horseback is keeping watch in addition to the doormen and hotel security. Fans are holding up signs saying things like WE ♥ ROS! and SYNC WITH ME, THEO! There's a press pen across the street, out of which a thicket of long lenses points in the direction of the hotel. There's even a satellite truck from one of the local TV stations parked near the press pen.

"Are you sure we're going to be able to get in?" I ask Eva. "They're going to think we're fans making up this internship to get into the hotel.

"Piece of cake!" she assures me.

I wonder if they serve cake in juvenile jail, because I have an uneasy feeling that's where we're going to end up. But the envelope addressed to Theo Downey scratches my skin, reminding me to keep my eyes on the prize, no matter what the obstacles.

"Follow me," Eva says, marching straight up to the security at the hotel door, and whipping out a piece of paper. "We're here to see Raphael Dario, the head of concierge services. We're the new interns."

I smile at the security guard with a confidence I don't feel. Like Mom says, *Fake it till you make it.*

"I don't know anything about this," he says. "Hold on."

He speaks into a radio. "I've got two teenage girls here claiming they're the new interns for Rafe Dario. Can you confirm it's legit? They have a printout of a letter from the president of the hotel, but given the situation . . ."

We can't hear the response in his earpiece, but he

says, "Thanks, I'll keep them here till you do."

I just hope he can't see my knees trembling, and I avoid looking over at Eva in case I give anything away. She seems totally relaxed, talking the security guard's ear off about how excited we are to start the internship.

Then he holds his earpiece and says, "Yeah, okay, I'll send them in." Handing the letter back to Eva, he says, "Inside and go straight to the concierge desk at the rear of the lobby. Someone will take you back to meet Mr. Dario."

"Thank you," I say as I exhale a breath I didn't even realize I was holding, both amazed and relieved that Eva is legit and we actually do have an internship. Especially when I see two security guards escorting a Retro of Sync fan out the front door of the hotel as we're going in. She's screaming, "IF I DON'T MEET THEO DOWNEY, I'LL DIEEEEEEEE!"

I know the feeling.

There's a woman behind the concierge desk wearing a dark blue suit. Her name tag reads BASIA, with American, Polish, and Russian flags underneath her name.

"Can I help you?" she asks with a slight accent.

"Eva Murgatroyd and Araminta Robicheaux," Eva says. "We're here to meet Mr. Dario for our internship."

She examines us like we're insects under a magnifying glass, then gestures for us to come around the back of the counter. "Follow me," she says, opening a door in the wood paneling.

It's like entering a different world. The lobby at Hotel Z is sleek and modern with a monochromatic color scheme and calming water features. Behind the door, it's noisy chaos.

"Why hasn't Lady Frostworth received her afternoon tea?" comes an angry shout from a doorway down the hall. "She's threatening to move to the Plaza!"

I hope that isn't Mr. Dario, but after telling us to leave our backpacks and coats in a closet, Basia leads us straight to that door and knocks on the jamb. "These are your new interns," she says. The way she says it, you'd think she was announcing relatives who showed up for Thanksgiving dinner without an invitation.

Mr. Dario is sitting behind a desk covered with paper. He rubs his forehead with his hand as Eva and I come in. "Just what I need, more teenagers running around this hotel," he mutters. "The legal liability alone . . ."

I get the impression that the decision to have us as interns wasn't one Mr. Dario got to make.

"Which one of you is Eva?" he says.

"That's me," Eva says, walking over to his desk.

"And you must be one of the friends."

"Good afternoon, Mr. Dario," I say, moving forward and sticking out my hand to shake, the way I was taught. "Araminta Robicheaux. But I prefer Minty."

"Minty?" he mutters under his breath. He shakes my hand for a brief instant, then says, "They told me I had to find work for three of you."

"Livvy's sick," Eva says. "She couldn't come."

His phone rings and he picks it up. "Rafe Dario, concierge services."

I'm amazed how his voice transforms from irritated to ingratiating in a matter of seconds.

"Oh yes, Lady Frostworth, I hope you found the cream tea to your satisfaction. I apologize for the delay and inconvenience."

I notice Eva's eyes scanning the papers on his desk while he says, "Oh yes, and to Snowball's, too, of course!"

Eva's eyes stop and she inches forward toward the desk to get a closer look. I'm worried that her less-than-subtle snooping is going to get us fired before we've even started.

"Of course we can send someone up to take Snowball for his walkies," Mr. Dario says. "In fact, just to make sure he's extra safe, I'll send two people. They'll be there momentarily. . . . Yes, very good, Lady Frostworth. Let me know if there's anything else we can do to be of service."

As soon as the phone is back in the cradle, his expression changes from fawning to frustrated.

"Well, that takes care of what to do with two middle-school-aged interns," he says. "I want you to head up to the Winston suite on the thirtieth floor and take Lady Frostworth's dog for a walk. To say that Her Ladyship loves Snowball more than her own children is an understatement. So don't let anything happen to him, or I will make sure you never get an internship in this town again. Understand?"

"We'll take great care of him," I promise Mr. Dario.

"Definitely," Eva says.

"And make sure you pick up after him if he poops," Mr. Dario says. "Otherwise the two-hundred-fifty-dollar fine will come out of your pay."

"We're interns. You're not paying us anything," Eva points out. "But don't worry, Daddy will pay my fine."

My daddy won't. He's too busy gallivanting around Europe with Mom, trying to achieve World Cleaning Product Domination. I get the sinking feeling that it will be me who has to pick up whatever Lady Frostworth's precious Snowball delivers.

We're almost out the door when he says, "Wait! You'll need a key card to get up to the thirtieth floor."

He takes one from his drawer and holds it out between his thumb and forefinger. "Guard this with your lives. This is a master key. Do not use it for any untoward purpose, and return it to me as soon as you have delivered Snowball back to Lady Frostworth."

Eva walks over and plucks the card key from his fingers. "No sweat, Mr. D." When she turns back to me, she is grinning from ear to ear.

"I couldn't have planned this better!" she says as we walk through the paneled door into the lobby and make a beeline for the elevator bank. "Not only do we have a master key, but now I know which suite Theo and the band are in."

"How?" I ask, pleasantly surprised that Eva's plan seems to be . . . working.

"He had a list of VIP guests on his desk. I read it upside down." She pushes the elevator button. "So we'll get Snowball, then head straight to the Buccellati suite, which is where the band is staying."

"But . . . what about Snowball's walkies?" I ask. "Doesn't he have to . . . you know . . . *go*?"

"We're going to walk him," Eva snaps. "Just not outside."

"But—"

"Minty, can you stop looking for problems and be more appreciative of my genius?" Eva says.

Whether Eva is actually a genius is a theory in need of proof, but I decide to keep that observation to myself until this is all over.

The elevator arrives and we get in. Eva waves the key card over the sensor, and when it flashes green, she presses the button for the thirtieth floor.

It's a silent ride for the first twenty floors; then Eva says, "Let me do the talking."

"Why you?" I ask. "I'm used to talking to lords and ladies. They were always hanging around at my grand-parents' place."

"My plan, my rules," Eva says.

I'm starting to wonder why I thought being friends with Eva was a good idea. At this point, I'm not sure I even *like* her.

When we get to the thirtieth floor, I follow Eva out of the elevator. An elegantly scripted sign on the wall tells us that the Winston, Tiffany, Cartier, and Mikimoto suites are to the right and the Van Cleef, Bucellati, Bulgari, and Asprey suites to the left.

"Remember, I do the talking," Eva reminds me.

I open my mouth to say something snarky, but then the envelope with the shoe sketches crinkles under my shirt, so I bite my tongue and nod. I just have to get through this plan, and then I'll happily join Livvy at the ex-friends-of-Eva table.

Eva knocks on the door of the Winston suite.

A formidable-looking older lady with snowy hair, wearing a cashmere sweater and tweed trousers, answers the door. She's got a small white fluff ball of a dog in her arms and some very un-sensible-looking shoes on her feet. They look like something the aunties would design.

"Good afternoon, Lady Frostworth. We're here to take Snowball for a walk," Eva says.

"Did you hear that, Snowball, my little chickadee?" Lady Frostworth coos, her upper-crust English accent still distinct despite the fact it's several octaves about her normal speaking voice. "These delightful young ladies are going to take you for your walkies."

Eva reaches to pet Snowball and he snaps at her fingers.

"Ow!" she says, drawing her hand back. "Bad dog!"

"Be nice, dear," Lady Frostworth says. It's unclear if she's directing this at Eva or Snowball.

"He almost drew blood!" Eva protests.

I slowly reach out a hand toward Snowball, making sure to approach him from below and not over his head, and to give him a chance to sniff me. His little pink tongue reaches out to lick my fingers, and his tail starts to wag. I pet his soft silky coat.

"Well, *someone* is a dog person," Lady Frostworth says, nodding her head approvingly. "Snowball always knows. He's a *very* good judge of character."

Eva shoots me a dirty look. It's pretty clear she doesn't like to be outshone in anything, even dog petting.

"Minty better take him, then," she says.

Lady Frostworth puts her precious pooch down and hands me his lead. "Make sure he does number one *and* number two," she says. "He always does both after we've shared our cream tea. He's very *regular*."

Regular has to do with pooping? Does that mean the aunties eat oatmeal so it will make them *poop*? Gross! Why would they tell me that?

Lady Frostworth reaches into her pocket and hands me a little green bag with a picture of a dog on it. "That's for his number two." Then she blows Snowball a kiss.

"Toddle off and do your business, my little poppet."

The door of the suite closes. Eva rolls her eyes and mutters, "Crazy old bat!" as she grabs my arm and starts dragging me down the hallway in the direction of the Buccellati suite.

Snowball trots along at my side, wagging his fluffy tail.

"Eva, how are we supposed to explain Snowball if Theo or the other band members are in the suite?" I ask.

Apparently this is a variable that Eva hasn't considered.

"You can wait down the hallway while I knock. If Theo answers, I'll talk to him first; then I'll hold Snowball while you talk to him."

I put the hand that's not holding the leash to my stomach, where the envelope containing my precious shoe designs rests against my skin.

"But what if he closes the door before I get to give him my designs?" I ask.

"Where are they?" Eva asks.

I pull the envelope out from under my shirt.

Eva grabs it from my fingers. "Just leave everything to me and wait here."

"But—"

"Trust me, Minty. I'm the genius, not you."

She marches off down the hallway. I look down at Snowball. He's got a quizzical expression on his furry face and starts trying to pull me in the direction of the elevator bank, like he's got the hotel walkies drill down and knows this isn't it.

"No, Snowball! We're waiting here!" I tell him. He turns back and lies down on the floor, his head between his front paws, looking up at me with reproachful brown puppy eyes.

Eva knocks on the door and calls out, "Concierge services." I'm about to look up to see if Theo answers so I can catch a glimpse of his utter and complete adorableness, when Snowball stands up, sniffs at the baseboard, and lifts his leg, spraying a new pattern on the wall.

"Snowball, no!" I hiss. I don't have anything to clean up with except the poop bag, and that's not exactly absorbent.

I glance around, and luckily, there aren't any witnesses to Snowball's liquid graffiti. Eva is also nowhere to be seen. Did I miss Theo? Is she inside talking to him without me?

I drag a reluctant Snowball over to the Buccellati suite, and I put my ear to the door. I don't hear any voices, so I knock softly. "Eva? Are you in there?"

There's no reply, so I knock a bit harder.

"Eva?"

I don't hear anything, but about ten seconds later the door swings open and Eva hisses, "Do you want the entire hotel to know we're in here?"

"No, but—"

She grabs my shirt and pulls me into the suite, almost slamming the door on Snowball's tail. He lets out a small yelp of shock, and I bend down to pet him and tell him, "It's okay, Snowball. We'll go out soon."

Then I turn to Eva and whisper, "Are they here?"

"No, they're not here," she says. Then, whipping out her phone, she shows me a selfie of herself lounging on a sofa wearing a leather jacket.

"Wait, is that the jacket Theo wore in the 'No One Dances with No One' video?" I ask, my heart beating a bit faster at the thought.

Eva nods, a smug smile on her face. "And in the 'You Find Me' and 'First Date of Forever' videos."

"Where is it?" I say. "I have to touch it."

I follow her into the living room at the center of the suite. Theo's jacket is lying on the sofa near the minibar. I walk over and reach tentative fingers to stroke the leather collar. "This collar touched Theo Downey's neck," I say. "And now I'm touching it, so it's almost as if *I've* touched Theo's neck too."

"I'm going into his bedroom," Eva says.

"How do you know which one is his?" I ask.

"Because I recognize some of the clothes in the closet," Eva says. "I told you, I'm his number one fan."

I decide to take off Snowball's leash, figuring there's nowhere he can go with the suite door shut, and at least that way he'll get some exercise running around. Then I follow Eva into Theo's room.

She's standing by the closet, hugging the T-shirt that he wore in the "Magic Romance" video as if Theo were still inside it.

I take out the bold yellow jacket he wore in the "Doorway to the Stars" video and waltz into the living room with it. Granny Robicheaux made me learn how to waltz "so that when it's your time, you'll have the important, necessary skills to marry your own Prince Charming." I tried telling her that nobody my age dances like that anymore, but she insisted.

I'm so busy waltzing with fantasy Theo that I accidentally hit my knee on the corner of the coffee table, which brings me back to painful reality.

"Ow!" I yell so loudly that Snowball barks. I look over and he's not only jumped up onto the sofa; he's hunched over on Theo's famous leather jacket, doing his number two.

"Snowball! NO!" I shout, startling him into jumping off the sofa.

It feels like all the breath is sucked out of my lungs. "Eva!" I gasp. "Snowball . . . jacket . . . help!"

As soon as Eva walks through the doorway, she stops and sniffs. "What is that awful smell? Did that little runt *poop* in Retro of Sync's *suite*?"

"It's even worse," I say, pointing to the sofa. "He pooped on *Theo's leather jacket.*"

"We better get out of here," Eva says. "Clean up that poop!" She runs for the door.

"Wait, why do I have to—"

Then, to my horror, I see Snowball following Eva out of the suite. "Snowball, no! STAY!"

He ignores me and runs into the hallway.

My heart races, and I can barely catch a breath as my panicked brain tries to figure out what to do. Should I clean up the poop or chase Snowball so nothing happens to him? As I try to inhale, I'm overwhelmed by poop smell and realize that if I go chase after Snowball without cleaning up, Mr. Dario will know that we misused his key card, since we were supposed to be walking the dog—outside. I have to dispose of the evidence, because I bet Theo's jacket cost a lot more than two hundred fifty dollars.

I pull the disposal bag Lady Frostworth gave me out of my back pocket, and, holding my nose with my other hand, I remove Snowball's odiferous offering from Theo's iconic jacket. Tying a knot in the bag, I glance around the room to remove any other signs that we've been there. The "Doorway to the Stars" jacket is on the floor where it fell when I hit my knee and noticed Snowball. I pick it up, and I'm putting it back in the closet when an earsplitting siren makes me jump. I hit my head on the door as a light starts flashing from a sprinkler sticking out of the ceiling. A computer voice shouts *"Fire! Fire! Fire! Please move to the nearest emergency exit and leave the hotel immediately! Fire! Fire! Fire!"*

This is officially turning out to be the Worst Day of My Life.

I close the closet and take one last look around Theo's room. Everything looks in place, so I run out, taking a final glance around the living room. It's only after I close the suite door behind me that I realize I didn't see my envelope anywhere.

I can't have gone through all this only to have Eva forget to leave it for Theo. I didn't see her carrying it when she left. But right now, I've got bigger problems, because Lady Farnsworth is heading my way with Snowball in her arms and fire in her eyes.

"You there!" she shouts. "How could you be so irresponsible with my precious? Poor little snookums was outside my suite door *completely unsupervised*! Someone could have stolen him! How could you?"

I decide now is a great time to exercise my Fifth Amendment right to avoid self-incrimination, so I run as fast as I can in the opposite direction. At this particular moment I'm actually glad to be living here instead of in Robicheaux, because that right doesn't exist in my grandfather's kingdom, and he's got the dungeons to prove it.

"Stop, you ghastly girl!" Lady Frostworth shouts. "I demand an answer!"

As I run toward the fire exit, one of my prized Trudy Neal flats slips off my foot. I want to go back to get it, but Lady Frostworth is hot on my trail with Snowball yapping in her arms. I'm forced to sacrifice my precious shoe on the altar of freedom—namely mine.

It better be worth it.

I open the fire-exit door and start making my way

down the stairs. There are *so many* of them—and I'm short a shoe and still carrying a bag of Snowball poop. I'm usually not a litterer, but I don't want to be caught with stinky, potentially incriminating evidence, so I throw the bag in a corner of the twenty-seventh-floor landing and keep going.

I text Eva, now that my hands are free.

Me: WHERE ARE YOU?

Me: Lady F was really mad about Snowball

She doesn't answer until I'm on the tenth floor and already feel a blister on my shoeless heel, as well as on my shoed toe.

Eva: I'm on my way home.

Eva: I saw Theo Downey in a bathrobe. And I got a selfie with him!!! ☺

Me: What? WHERE?

Eva: In the elevator. He was on the way back to the suite after spending time at the pool.

Eva: I talked to him and got the selfie—even though his security guy was being a jerk about it. Then I got off and did the one thing I knew would rescue you.

Me: YOU pulled the fire alarm?

Me: Do you realize I've had to walk down THIRTY FLIGHTS OF STAIRS?

Eva: Better that than getting caught in Theo's suite with a poopy leather jacket.

Eva: Oh, by the way, I've got your backpack and coat.

Eva: I ran in to get mine when the fire alarm was going off, and figured you'd need it tomorrow.

She's got my backpack and coat? That means . . . I have no money, no coat, and only one shoe.

Me: I need it NOW! How am I supposed to get home? YOU'VE GOT MY WALLET!

Eva: I don't know. Call your aunties.

Me: They'll want to know why I was here. And why I only have one shoe!

Eva: How did you lose a shoe?

Me: Running away from a very angry Lady Frostworth, who found Snowball ALONE outside the door of her suite.

Me: And what did you do with my envelope? I didn't see it in the ROS suite.

I'm almost to the ground floor by the time she answers.

Eva: It's there.

Eva: I put it in a Hotel Z envelope so it looked more official.

Eva: That way Theo's more likely to open it.

Eva: You can thank me later.

Thanking Eva is the last thing on my mind. Right

now I'll be happy if I never see her again—except to get my coat and backpack back, that is.

I'm going to have to call the aunties—but which one? I decide to call Aunt Margaux, because after watching her deal with the angry New York taxi driver, I think she'd be better in a crisis than Aunt Lottie.

"When are you getting home? I've got all the cookie ingredients ready to go," Margaux says when she picks up. "And what's that horrible noise in the background?"

"It's a fire alarm. Aunt Margaux, I've got a major crisis. It's a long story, but I'm stuck at the Hotel Z with no money or coat, and I don't know how to get home."

"Hang tight, I'm on my way," she says, without even asking why I'm here and what happened to my money and coat.

"Thank you, Aunt Margaux! You're a lifesaver," I say, my heart filling with gratitude.

"But Minty, we *will* be talking about this after I rescue you," she warns. "See you shortly."

She hangs up, and my gratitude mingles with a sense of impending doom.

I walk out the door from the stairwell to the main lobby, and I wonder, if I walk really slowly toward the front door, will the fire alarm will be called off before I have to go outside without a coat? That's when I hear "YOOOOOOOU!" bellowed from across the lobby, and I see Mr. Dario marching toward me, his face red with fury.

So much for staying warm—I'm going to make like a tree and leave.

I'm almost at the door when I feel a heavy hand on my shoulder.

"Not so fast, young lady," Mr. Dario says, spinning me around to face him. "How did Lady Frostworth's dog end up running loose on the thirtieth floor? She's threatening to leave the hotel and never stay with us again. Even worse, she said she's going to leave bad reviews for us on every travel site on both sides of the Atlantic!"

I try to come up with an explanation that isn't going to get me into even more trouble. "I um . . . he um . . ."

My mind goes blank—but then I catch a glimpse of a very familiar famous face over Mr. Dario's shoulder.

"Th-that's Th-Theo Downey!" I stammer. He's wearing a swanky bathrobe with HOTEL Z embroidered on the right chest pocket, and his hair is wet. He looks a little smaller in real life than he does on the Internet, but just as gorgeous.

"I knew I shouldn't have agreed to take you two on

as interns," Mr. Dario mutters. "I told them it wouldn't end well."

Then, pasting an ingratiating smile on his face, he starts toward Theo but turns back to me and says, "And by the way, you're fired."

On the bright side, this means I don't have to worry about coming back for the internship I wasn't sure I really wanted. On the not-so-bright side, will Mr. Dario spread word that I'm an irresponsible dog loser?

My future job prospects have definitely taken a turn for the worse.

I go outside and shiver with the hotel guests and the Retro of Sync fans, waiting for Aunt Margaux to save me.

I know exactly when Theo walks out the door in his bathrobe, because the screaming is deafening. He goes over to the barricade and takes selfies with fans and signs autographs. I would have been better off standing in the cold to meet him with the rest of his fans instead of agreeing to Eva's outlandish plan.

A dog barks and I see Lady Frostworth standing not that far from me in the crowd, with a yapping Snowball in her arms.

I slink backward to try to hide behind a tall guy in a

business suit, and my shoeless foot steps in something wet.

I look down, and it appears to be dog pee.

Just when I thought things couldn't get worse. I hope Aunt Margaux gets here before I get myself into any more trouble.

Chapter Eight

AUNT MARGAUX TEXTS ME TO TELL ME she's around the corner in a black sedan, because the police are diverting traffic away from the Hotel Z. I want to hop around the corner so I don't step in any other gross things with my bare foot, but Trudy Neal flats weren't made for hopping. So I end up limping to the corner with my eyes on the ground to avoid disgusting street stuff.

There are like twenty black sedans lined up on Sixth Avenue and I wonder how I'm supposed to figure out which one contains my aunt, when I hear Margaux bellowing, "MINTY! OVER HERE!" and I see her standing by a car all the way down the block.

I'm so busy looking at her that I forget to look at the ground, and I step in something squishy.

Omigod, please don't let it be poop!

Spoiler alert: It is.

My Worst Day Ever just got even worse.

Tears start welling in my eyes as I run to Aunt Margaux and throw myself in her bony arms.

"Aunt Margaux, I'm so glad you're here!" I sniff into her faux-leopard coat.

She sniffs too, but for a different reason. "What is that disgusting smell?" she says, looking down at my feet. "And why are you only wearing one shoe?"

"I stepped in dog poop," I say. "Pee, too. I'll tell you the rest in the car."

"You're not getting into this car with that poopy foot," she says. "Where's my knife? I'll have to cut it off."

"WHAT?" I exclaim, getting reading to run for my life.

"Joke," she says with a grin. She reaches into the back of the sedan and rummages in her purse. I hear her asking the driver if he has tissues. Then she tells me to sit on the back seat "but keep that stinky foot outside or I *will* cut it off."

She pours half a bottle of hand sanitizer on my foot and then uses a big handful of tissues to wipe off the offending substances. I still plan to use some Crud Crusher™ on my foot when I get home, but at least I feel slightly less gross in the meantime.

Aunt Margaux walks to the trash can on the corner to throw out the disgusting tissues and uses the rest of the sanitizer to clean her hands; then we both slide into the back seat of the car. "Back home now," she tells the driver, and then, turning to me, she says, "Okay, Minty—spill. Right now. What mischief have you been up to?"

I tell her about my favorite band's sold-out concerts, and the contest I just missed the deadline for, and Eva's plan to meet Theo Downey to get my contest entries in front of him so I would have a chance to win tickets.

What I don't tell her is that the contest involved designing shoes, because despite this complete disaster of a day, I still have a tiny grain of hope that someday I might be known for something I do myself, not just because I'm Mom and Dad's daughter or the aunties' niece.

"None of this explains why you ended up with no money, no coat, and one shoe," Aunt Margaux says. "What's the rest of the story?"

"Our first job as interns was to walk Lady Frostworth's dog, Snowball," I say.

"Lady Frostworth? She's one of our customers!" Aunt Margaux says.

"I thought those were Comfortably Ever After shoes," I say with a gulp. "You better not tell her you're my aunt, or she won't be your customer any longer."

"Minty . . . what did you do?" Aunt Margaux says, her eyes narrowing. She looks like she's considering cutting my foot off for real.

I confess how Eva said this was our chance to get my designs in front of Theo, and how Snowball pooped on Theo Downey's famous leather jacket.

To my surprise, she starts guffawing with laughter.

"It's not funny," I wail. "It was horrible! Eva told *me* to clean it up while she ran away, and she left the door open and Snowball ran after her, and I didn't know if I should chase him and leave the poop or stay to clean it up!"

Aunt Margaux wipes her eyes. "So I'm assuming you stayed to clean up?"

I nod.

"Of course you did—you're Ella's daughter," she says with a chuckle. "Was that when you stepped in it?"

"No, I had to run away from Lady Frostworth, because she was so mad about finding Snowball alone in the hallway. I was running away from her when my shoe slid off, and I was afraid to risk going back to get it," I explain. "Oh, and Eva pulled the fire alarm because she bumped into Theo Downey in the elevator and he was on his way back to the suite. But she waited until *after* she took a selfie with him."

Aunt Margaux isn't amused when she hears this. She's shaking her head, her lips compressed in a thin line as I tell her the rest of my tale of woe.

"So I got fired from the internship, and the worst part is that I'm in all this trouble and I'm not even sure if Eva left my designs in the suite for Theo like she said she would."

"Well, Minty, you've managed to get yourself into quite a pickle," Aunt Margaux says.

"Tell me something I *don't* know," I say.

"When do they announce the contest winners?" Aunt Margaux asks.

"Tomorrow at noon," I say, feeling more desperate by the minute. "I just wanted a chance to win. And now I'm not even going to get that."

"You don't know that for sure," Aunt Margaux says. "Your friend could have left your entry for Theo to find."

"The thing is . . . I'm starting to wonder if she really *is* my friend," I say. "I mean, she ditched me at the hotel and took my coat and backpack with her. That's why I was stuck there without money or a MetroCard."

My aunt puts her arm around me and hugs me tight. "Sometimes it takes a bad experience to figure out who your *real* friends are," she says. "Take it from Lottie and me."

"Why, did you have friends who encouraged you to do stupid things?"

"Worse than that—it was our mother," Aunt Margaux says. "Unfortunately, we didn't realize it until *after* we'd mutilated our feet to try and fit them into that stupid glass slipper. It was all because she wanted to be the royal mother-in-law."

She lets out a bitter laugh. "We were mean to Ella to earn Mother's approval, and we hurt ourselves trying to impress your dad so he'd marry one of us." I feel her exhale a big sigh. "If we'd spent our energy doing what we really loved, we'd probably be at the top of the rap charts by now. People would be doing stupid things like you did just to get tickets to *our* concerts."

I snort. As stressed out as I am, I can't help it. "Aunt Margaux, have you ever listened to *real* rap music?"

She gives me a lopsided grin. "Okay, maybe not at the *top* of the rap charts," she admits. "Maybe the top fifty."

"Top one hundred—maybe," I say.

Aunt Margaux takes my hand. "I was really looking forward to you teaching me how to make Ella's oatmeal raisin cookies this afternoon," she says. "I guess that's not going to happen today either. We're going to be too busy trying to figure out how to get you out of this mess."

I didn't know that it was possible to feel worse than I already did, but knowing that Aunt Margaux dropped everything to come rescue me after I blew her off to do something stupid—achievement unlocked.

We ride the rest of the way back in silence, each lost in our thoughts of what might have been.

As soon as we walk into the apartment, Aunt Lottie comes out of the living room, hands aflutter.

"Minty, there was something on the news about that Theo Downer guy you like. There was a hullabalo at his hotel this afternoon!"

Hullabalo is one way of putting it, I guess.

"Well, fancy that," Aunt Margaux says, giving me a stern look. "Who would have thought?"

"It's Downey," I tell Aunt Lottie.

"I recorded the segment for you," Aunt Lottie says, ushering me into the living room, where an image of the Hotel Z is frozen on the screen. "Here, Minty, sit." As she pushes me down onto the sofa, she notices my one bare foot. "Why are you only wearing one shoe?" she asks, her brow knit with confusion.

"You don't want to know," Aunt Margaux says, her voice as dry as a desert.

"Yes, I do!" Aunt Lottie protests.

"Please don't fight," I beg them. "Can we just watch the news thing?"

The aunties glare at each other, but Aunt Lottie pushes play on the remote.

"Now we turn to Channel Five reporter Joanie Phillips, who is on the scene at the Hotel Z."

"Thanks, Katie. The exclusive midtown Hotel Z had to be evacuated this afternoon. Guests were allowed to return to their rooms after the police and fire departments determined that it was a false alarm. Among the famous guests—chart-topping band Retro of Sync."

They show footage of Theo posing with fans in his robe.

"Fans camping outside hoping to catch sight of lead singer Theo Downey got a bit more than they bargained for, as he emerged from the lobby in a hotel robe."

Cut to fans screaming.

"One thirteen-year-old fan had to be taken away in

an ambulance after fainting from excitement," Joanie Phillips continues. "Hotel officials say they have a lead on who pulled the alarm, an offense which carries a potential penalty of up to a year in prison and a fine of ten thousand dollars. More news as it develops. Back to you, Katie."

Aunt Lottie turns off the TV. "This wouldn't have anything to do with the 'hypothetical' question you asked the other day about doing something stupid to get a guy's attention, would it, Minty?"

"Oh, we can safely say it would," Aunt Margaux says before I have a chance to answer. "I'd hate for Ella to get a call from the police while she's on this super-important business trip in Europe."

"It would make us look really bad," Aunt Lottie says, nodding her head in agreement. "Like we can't take care of you for even a few days without you getting into trouble."

"Just when Ella finally started to trust us," Aunt Margaux says.

Guilt weighs down on my chest.

"Did you pull the fire alarm?" Aunt Lottie asks.

"Would I be dumb enough to do something like that?" I ask. I mean it as a rhetorical question, but my aunts both nod yes so vigorously I wouldn't be surprised if they need a chiropractor tomorrow.

"Remember, dear, you're talking to *us*. We're the poster children for doing something dumb to impress a guy," Aunt Lottie says.

"Yes," Aunt Margaux agrees. "We hoped you'd learned from our mistakes."

"I have!" I protest, despite all evidence to the contrary.

Aunt Margaux gives me serious side eye. "Oh yes? How about you tell your aunt Lottie what you got up to this afternoon."

I'm forced to fill Aunt Lottie in on my official Worst Day Ever.

"But I swear, it wasn't me who pulled the fire alarm," I say, getting out my phone and pulling up the texts from Eva. "See—Eva admits that she did."

Aunt Lottie looks at my phone and then hands it to Margaux. "What does it say, Marge? I can't read anything without my glasses."

"It's a confession, all right," Aunt Margaux says. She takes a screenshot and texts it to herself.

"They say they have a lead . . . what happens if it points to me?" I say. "I'm too young to go to jail! And I definitely don't have ten thousand dollars!"

"Don't worry," Aunt Margaux says. "Leave that to us." She glances down at my foot.

"In the meantime, why don't you go wash that foot," she says. "Use hot water to kill any germs you might have picked up from the street."

"But don't burn yourself. We've had enough excitement for one day without a trip to the ER," Aunt Lottie adds.

I head to the bathroom to try to get the rest of the New York City sidewalk crud off my feet. After filling the tub with the hottest water I can stand, I put in my foot, and despite Aunt Margaux's efforts with hand sanitizer and tissues, I still see gray-black dirt swirling out from it. Ugh, will my foot ever feel clean again?

I take a washcloth and load it up with some of Mom's Crud Crusher™, then scrub furiously. I'm impressed with how well the Crud Crusher™ works. My foot is clean again in minutes. If I didn't want to keep this nightmare a secret from my parents, I'd tell Mom that.

Still, I'm worried about what Aunt Margaux said about "germs you might have picked up from the street." What kind of germs does she mean?

I dry my now-clean foot with a towel and search: "Can you catch diseases from going barefoot in New York City?"

To my dismay, the answer is a definite yes: everything

from fungal diseases like athlete's foot and plantar warts to skin diseases and hookworm. *Ugh!* I feel sweat trickling from my forehead into my eyes, and I worry that it might be the first sign of a death-inducing fever. If I die because of Eva Murgatroyd, I vow to be a very angry and persistent ghost haunting her from the afterlife.

Chapter Nine

FORTUNATELY, I LIVE THROUGH THE NIGHT
without contracting any deadly diseases or having the
police show up at my door to take me to juvenile jail for
a crime that I didn't commit. I guess there's still a chance
of developing deadly disease symptoms if there's an incu-
bation period, but I've got enough to worry about—like
getting through seeing Eva at school and the announcement of the contest winner at noon.

Then I pick up my phone and see the texts from Mom
and Dad.

Mom: We got a phone call from the office. The NEW
YORK POLICE DEPARTMENT called looking for our daughter

in connection with a false fire alarm that resulted in the Hotel Z having to be evacuated.

Dad: I knew we shouldn't have left you with Lottie and Margaux.

Mom: We're taking the next flight home. By the time you get this, we'll be in the air.

Dad: PS. You're grounded.

This is not good.

I hear a shriek from the spare room.

It sounds like the aunties got a text from my parents too.

A minute later they appear in my doorway, Aunt Lottie in a nightie with her hair in curlers, and Aunt Margaux in flannel pajamas, her hair all over the place.

"Minty! Your parents are coming home!" Aunt Margaux says, her face panicked.

"We don't know how things are going to go," Aunt Lottie says, gazing at me with sad brown eyes.

Aunt Margaux clears her throat. "Lottie and I just want you to know that we . . . we think of you like the daughter we never had."

My aunts look uncharacteristically solemn. It scares me.

"You make it sound like we're never going to see each other again," I say.

"Ella thinks we're bad influences on you," Aunt

Lottie says, her eyes glistening with unshed tears.

Aunt Margaux gives a bitter-sounding chuckle. "Maybe it's a good thing we never had children, considering we couldn't even manage to look after you for a week without it ending badly."

Guilt blooms in my chest. "That's not your fault!" I exclaim. "It's mine."

Aunt Lottie shakes her head sadly. "Ella doesn't see it that way. She left us in loco parentis."

"She and Dad left me to go to Europe a week after uprooting me from my life in Robicheaux," I point out. "It's not like they're parents of the year, is it?"

Despite their sadness, the aunties look at each other and nod approvingly.

"The girl's got sass," Margaux says. Unlike my parents, she makes it sound like that's a good thing.

"I mean it," I say, wanting them to be serious. "You were great in loco parentises. You didn't do anything wrong." Aunt Lottie's eyes are welling up again, so I add: "Well, except for making me dance in that video."

Aunt Margaux laughs. "You and Lottie are both . . . shall we say *rhythm challenged*?" she says.

"*What?*" Lottie exclaims. "Robbie says that when he had to dance with you, he needed a pair of steel-toed boots because you stepped on his feet so much."

"No, that was what he said about *you*," Margaux says.

Aunt Lottie opens her mouth to retort, and I sense they're starting to wind up into a full-scale argument.

"Time out!" I shout. "What are we going to do?"

The aunts look at me sheepishly.

"We'll think of something," Aunt Margaux says. "I don't know what yet, but we'll figure it out."

"She's right," Aunt Lottie says. "When we put our heads together, we can solve any problem."

"You get ready for school and we'll make you breakfast," Aunt Margaux tells me. "'Never face the day without a good breakfast,' Ella used to say. And that's when she was being forced to cook ours before we went to school."

"*I'll* make the breakfast," Aunt Lottie says. "We've got enough to deal with this morning without having to call New York's Bravest."

Aunt Margaux scowls at her. "That only happened once!"

"It only happened once *in this apartment*," Aunt Lottie says. "I've lost track of how many times it's happened at home."

"Well, I'm supervising," Aunt Margaux says, stomping down the hallway to the kitchen.

"Okay, Marge!" Aunt Lottie calls after her. Then she winks at me. "As long as she doesn't touch the oven or the microwave."

"I heard that!" Aunt Margaux shouts from the kitchen. "And stop calling me Marge!"

I get dressed and put on my favorite pair of boots, which I "borrowed" from Mom's closet. It's my prerogative for having inherited her tiny feet.

By the time I get to the kitchen, Aunt Lottie has prepared a huge stack of pancakes without having to call the fire department, a fact she doesn't hesitate to tell my other aunt once every thirty seconds—at least until Margaux threatens to pour the jug of maple syrup over her head.

We all tuck into their fluffy deliciousness. When I'm so full I couldn't eat another bite, I ask: "So what are we going to do?"

"We've got most of the day to think about it," Aunt Margaux says. "We don't know what flight Ella and Robbie are on, but I checked and there's no way they'll get back before you get home from school."

"Okay. But I hope you think of something," I say, getting up from the table and putting my dishes in the dishwasher. "I've got to get going."

"Minty, wait!" Aunt Lottie exclaims, going to the fridge. "Today's not going to be an easy one," she says, holding up a paper lunch bag. "I made this for you last night. It's a very nutritious lunch." She smiles. "Well, except for the cupcake from Patisserie Bon Gateaux. That's not nutritious, but it's definitely necessary."

I take the lunch bag and look at the elaborate patchwork of affirmations she's drawn on the bag: things like *We hit the jackpot when Ella and Robbie had you* and *Shine your light—it's bright and beautiful* and a picture of two snow ladies who bear a striking resemblance to the aunties saying *We love you and that's snow joke!*

A rush of warmth in my chest makes the weight that's been crushing it down lighter. I throw my arms around Aunt Lottie's neck.

"Thank you, Aunt!" I say, and she gives me a big hug before releasing me

"I love you, Minty," Lottie says.

I hug her tight.

"I love you more," Aunt Margaux says, pulling me away from Aunt Lottie and in to her bony chest.

"No you don't!" Aunt Lottie says.

"Of course I do!" Margaux retorts.

I leave them arguing about who bears the greater love for me, Araminta Robicheaux, the niece who brought the Wrath of Robert and Ella down on their heads. I don't feel like I deserve it right now, but I'm so grateful the aunties are in my life. I hope my parents let them stay.

Livvy is outside waiting when I get to school.

"So how did it go?" she asks. "Were you there when the hotel had to be evacuated? There were videos of Theo in a bathrobe all over YouTube."

I should have gone to Starcups with Dakota instead.

"You're so lucky you decided to ditch," I tell her. "I wish I had."

I look around to make sure no one is listening.

"Eva pulled the fire alarm. And the police think I did it, and now my parents are coming home from Europe because they think the aunties are a bad influence."

"The police think you did it? That stinks!"

"I was stuck in Theo's suite cleaning up dog poop, and Eva ditched me there. Then she ran into Theo in the elevator. I had to walk down thirty flights of stairs, and Lady Frostworth says she's never going to stay at the

Hotel Z again because we left Snowball unattended, and I got fired from the internship that Eva's dad arranged, and I lost one of my vintage Trudy Neal flats and stepped in dog poop on the street with my bare foot, and I'm afraid of catching a communicable disease now, and my parents might not let me see the aunties ever again, but Eva actually thinks I should *thank* her!"

Livvy's eyes are wide. "It sounds like it went even worse than I thought it would," she says.

"I went along with Eva's plan because it was the only way to get my designs considered for the contest," I tell her. "But Eva told me to give her my entry, and I don't even know if she left it in the hotel room for Theo Downey to find."

"Oh, Minty," Livvy says, shaking her head.

"I don't know what she did with it," I say with a sigh. "And unless I win, I'll never know the truth, because it's not like I can believe Eva anymore."

"They're announcing the winner at noon," Livvy says. "During lunch."

"It probably won't be me, and with my luck I'll end up at the police station instead of the concert," I mutter gloomily.

"Whatever happens, your designs are really good," Livvy says, squeezing my arm. "Way better than anything Eva could do. She's not so great at drawing."

"Hey, Minty!"

Eva is hurrying toward us, carrying my coat and backpack.

"Speak of the devil," Livvy says to me under her breath.

"Here's your stuff," Eva says breezily, dumping it into my arms. "Livvy, you really missed out." She shoves her phone under Livvy's nose. "Look, I got a selfie with Theo!"

Livvy casts a quick glance at the photo and then glares at Eva. "You got a selfie with him and left Minty to take the fall."

"What are you—"

"But that was probably the plan all along, wasn't it?" Livvy cuts Eva off. "Get the new girl to take the rap so you could get what you want, right?"

Eva's eyes narrow, showing a flash of anger, but then she schools her features into an expression of innocent shock. "How can you even think that?" she says. "I thought we were friends."

"Yeah, such good friends that the minute I didn't do

what you wanted, you disinvited me from going to the concert," Livvy says.

"What?" I exclaim. I turn to Eva. "How could you? Livvy was looking forward to it!"

Livvy nods, looking straight at Eva, who is stone-faced. "Yes, I was." Then she turns and looks me in the eye. "She could have just offered you my ticket instead of encouraging you to take all those risks yesterday, but I'll bet you a life-size Theo Downey poster that she didn't."

I shake my head slowly.

"That's because you were always disposable," Livvy continues. "And I have proof."

"What do you mean, proof?" Eva snaps.

Livvy takes out her own phone and hands it to me. "You forgot to take me out of the group chat when you bragged to Hunter, Connor, and Ginny about using Minty because she was so gullible," she tells Eva.

I look down at the chat convo.

Eva: Connor, you owe me ALL THE COOKIES.

Selfie of Eva with Theo is attached.

Ginny: OMG. You met him? How?!!!

Hunter: He's shorter than he looks on TV.

Connor: I bet it's a cardboard cutout.

Eva: It isn't! Look, here's a picture I snuck of him in the elevator before I got off.

Picture of Theo Downey in a Hotel Z bathrobe with his bodyguard glaring into the camera.

Ginny: Spill the deets! How did you get into the hotel? I heard the security was 100%

Eva: Daddy got an internship at the hotel for me and that new girl, Minty.

Eva: Livvy, too, but she chickened out.

Eva: That got us in.

Connor: Is that why you were being so nice to the new girl all of a sudden?

Hunter: I thought it was because you wanted to be in another commercial

Eva: I do. But I also needed to have a fall girl, in case anything went wrong.

Eva: And it did. But my plan worked, because everyone thinks it was her who caused the evacuation. The owner of the Hotel Z told Daddy that yesterday.

I stare at Eva, trembling with anger. "You were planning on leaving me behind all along? How *could* you?"

"Because she's so used to getting everything she wants, that's how," Livvy says.

"Did you even leave my designs for Theo to find, or was that a lie too?" I ask Eva.

"I did leave them." She protests so vigorously that I'm about to believe her. "I told you, I just put them in a hotel envelope so he'd be more likely to open it!"

But one look at Livvy's skeptical impression reminds me of the danger of trusting a word that comes out of Eva's mouth.

"They're probably in a garbage can somewhere," I say, my heart weighting my chest. My hope of going to the concert is practically nonexistent, and I'm in serious trouble.

"I don't know why you're complaining. I didn't force you to come with me," Eva says, lifting her chin. "You have free will."

#Thatawkwardmomentwhen the person you're mad at makes a point.

"But you got me to go along with your plan under false pretenses," I snap.

"Well, you got to see Theo Downey," Eva says, shrugging. "Don't complain you didn't get what you said you wanted."

As she flounces off, I wish I could go home, crawl under the covers, and magically transport myself back to Robicheaux, where my life was so much simpler.

That's when it hits me—the reason everything was so much easier for me there was exactly because of my name and family legacy. In other words, the very thing from which I've been trying so hard to escape.

I avoid Eva's table at lunch, instead inviting Livvy to sit with me. Together we take the long way around the cafeteria to join Aria, Sophie, and Nina. Livvy with her tray of cafeteria food and me with my brown paper bag lovingly packed and decorated by Aunt Lottie.

I glance over at Eva. I can tell she's talking about Livvy and me, because she keeps looking in our direction and laughing, like we're the punch line of some joke.

Why did I ever think that being one of "Eva's Elites" was a good idea?

"Did you see what happened at the Hotel Z yesterday?" Sophie asks.

"Funny you should mention that," Livvy says.

"Why?" Aria asks.

"I was there," I explain.

"What? No way!" Nina exclaims. "You have to tell us *everything*."

"Yeah, don't leave out *anything*," Sophie adds.

I repeat the sorry tale of my sad adventures at the

Hotel Z. Every time I tell people, I feel worse about having trusted Eva.

"The things you wanted the band to see . . . were those the designs you showed us in Couture Club?" Aria says.

I nod.

"I didn't get to see them," Sophie says. "I'm too hopeless with a needle to be in Couture Club. You'd think *I* was Sleeping Beauty's daughter, not Aria."

I reach into my bag to find my sketchbook so I can show Sophie the designs. It's not there.

"Where is it?" I mutter, trying to remember the last time I saw it.

"Where's what?" Sophie asks.

"My sketchbook. I'm sure it was in my bag. I always keep it with me in case I get an idea."

"Minty," Livvy says, and the tone of her voice makes my heart sink. "Didn't Eva have your backpack last night?"

"Yeah, but what's that got to do with anything?"

She points to the time on her phone. It's 11:59.

I feel like the nutritious turkey sandwich Aunt Lottie made me is about to reappear.

"No . . . she wouldn't . . ." I groan, knowing full well that Eva would.

"There's a live stream of the announcement," Livvy

says. "Here." She holds her phone so that we can all see it. There's an empty table with four chairs, in front of a backdrop of Retro of Sync's latest album cover. A banner in front of the table reads: DESIGN CONTEST WINNER ANNOUNCEMENT.

I glance over at Eva. She's staring at her phone the same way that we're staring at Livvy's. Then I look over at the cafeteria clock. Both hands point to twelve.

On Livvy's phone, the members of Retro of Sync file into the room, amid the clicking of what sounds like hundreds of camera shutters. Theo is wearing the jacket that Snowball pooped on. I hope I cleaned it off well enough that he doesn't end up with any of the poop-borne diseases I read about on the Internet. I've got enough on my conscience already.

"Hey, Syncos," Theo says. "Guess you're all excited to hear who won the design contest and gets the VIP experience for the concert tomorrow night, right?"

"It's more like dread now," I mutter.

"What's in the VIP experience?" Jimmy Strage, the ROS guitarist asks, even though he probably knows.

"Well, Jimmy, it's just a boatload of awesome," Theo says. "A stretch limo from Luxury Limos will come to take you and your BFFs to the concert, where you'll be ushered to a box with the best view in the arena. There you'll enjoy delicious eats catered by Enchanted Soirées as you watch the show."

"What about the backstage passes?" asks bassist Chad Apollo.

"How could I forget?" Theo says. "Yes, the winner will get backstage passes to meet us after the concert."

"So go on, then," says drummer Tom Donham. "Tell us who won!"

"There were so many great entries," Theo says. "We had a hard time choosing. But ultimately the winner was a last-minute entry delivered directly to our suite."

Livvy and I stare at each other, and my heart starts beating like a race car during the grand prix. "Omigosh!" Livvy says. "Maybe she did give them your designs after all—"

"Congratulations to our design-contest winner," Theo continues. "Eva Murgatroyd!"

Eva's scream of "I WON!" cuts through the cafeteria.

I feel like I'm in a waking nightmare, one that only gets worse as Eva's winning designs are flashed onto the screen of Livvy's phone.

"Those are *my* designs," I say, grabbing the phone

from Livvy's hand. "Eva passed *my* designs off as *hers* and *they won*."

"Wow," Aria says. "That's even worse than what Jesse tried to do to me on *Teen Couture*."

"Aria, he tried to kill you," Sophie says. "If he hadn't messed up the spell . . . I mean, isn't *death* worse than stealing Minty's designs?"

Livvy is shaking her head. She seems as stunned as I am. "I know Eva, and even I didn't think she'd go *that* far," she says.

"Minty, we have to do something." Nina says.

"Yeah, we can't let her get away with this," Aria agrees.

As I watch people go up to congratulate Eva, I'm paralyzed by competing emotions—pride because Retro of Sync chose my designs as the winner, and anger because I'm not going to enjoy the prize because Eva stole them. She already had tickets to Saturday's concert—why did she have to take this from me?

"You're right," I say.

"What are you going to do?" Livvy asks.

"I don't know yet," I admit. "But I'm going to think of something."

🦢

I decide to wait till after school to confront Eva. I catch up to her in the hallway as she's walking to the front door, grab her arm, and say: "We need to talk."

Her eyes shift away from me. "What could we possibly have to talk about?"

"Oh please, you know," I say. "And you're going to want to do this in private."

"Fine," she sighs, tossing her head. "In there." She points to the nearest bathroom. We both look for feet under the stall doors. As soon as it's clear no one else is in there, I say, "You stole my designs."

"You can't prove that," Eva says. She turns to the mirror and starts fluffing her hair.

"I could—if you hadn't stolen my sketchbook, too," I say.

"Like I said, you can't prove it," she says, giving the mirror a sly smile, her eyes shining with triumph. "You and Livvy can have a little losers party while I'm VIP-ing it at the concert tomorrow."

The unfairness crashes over me, threatening to drown me in a wave of despair. How can I prove they're my sketches when Eva's stolen my sketchbook?

I surreptitiously push record on my phone while she reapplies her lip gloss.

"When did you decide to steal my designs?" I ask.

"Don't you mean *my* designs?" Eva says.

"Hypothetically speaking, of course," I say.

"If I *had* done it, I would have decided to do it when you showed Livvy and me your sketches," Eva says. "I would have realized you were so desperate to win the contest that you'd go along with anything I told you might make it happen, and you'd be stupid enough to hand over your designs to me if you thought I could get them in front of Theo."

A scream wells up in my throat, but I hold it back.

"Then, as soon as I was in the suite, I took the designs and your note out of the envelope and put them into a hotel envelope, with a note from me," Eva says. She laughs. "Oops. I mean that's totally *not* what happened, because they're my designs."

"Why?" I ask. "Why would you do that to me? You already had tickets."

Eva laughs. "Because I can, Minty."

She puckers her lips and blows herself a kiss in the mirror. Then she heads for the bathroom door. "Well, this has been a nice little chat, but I've got things to do, and Retro of Sync concerts to see."

She opens the door to leave.

"Wait!" I call out. "What if I can prove those are my designs?"

Eva closes the door and takes a few steps toward me so that we're almost nose to nose.

"What do you mean?" she says, her eyes narrowed. "How?"

I don't have the faintest clue how I'm going to prove it yet, but I'm not giving up without a fight.

"I'm not going to tell you how," I say, hoping that I can figure it out in the very near future. "But I *will* prove it."

Eva's entire demeanor changes, like she's flicked a switch to go back to being a fake friend.

"Minty, we seem to have gotten off on the wrong foot," she says. "How about I give you my original tickets?"

"You mean the ones you already had before you stole my designs to get the VIP package?" I say. "Those tickets?"

Eva raises an eyebrow, as if she's confused by my lack of immediate gratitude. "I thought you wanted to see

Retro of Sync. I'm willing to give you tickets. You're getting what you wanted."

"While you steal what I would have won," I point out. "Nope. No deal."

As soon as she realizes that I'm not going to be bought off with tickets, she drops all pretense of being friends again.

"Fine. Your loss, Minty. Good luck proving that they're your designs before the concert."

With that, she flounces out of the bathroom, leaving me trying to figure out how on earth I'm going to make good on my threat.

Chapter Ten

AFTER EVA LEAVES, I TAKE MY PHONE OUT to make sure the recording worked. There's a flurry of texts from the aunties.

AuntieM: Your parents get into JFK at 4:55 p.m.

AuntieM: They want you home and us gone.

AuntieL: We'll miss you, Minty.

AuntieM: Keep on being you!

AuntieL: Because you are the best niece we could have ever imagined.

AuntieM: Even better than we imagined.

AuntieL: Is that even possible, Marge?

AuntieM: Of course it's possible! And how many times

do I have to tell you to stop calling me Marge!

Their argument continues for another screen's worth of texts.

I didn't want the aunties to come, but now I'm devastated to see them go—especially because it's my fault.

My thumbs hover over the screen as I try to figure out what to say. Instead I put the phone in my bag, deciding to wait until the right words come to me. I can't face the thought of going back to the auntieless apartment and waiting there for my parents to come home and punish me. Starcups seems like a much better idea. Maybe a cup of hot chocolate will help me figure out solutions to my many problems. It certainly can't hurt, right?

As I'm walking down the street, I hear, "Hey, Araminta, wait up!"

I stop and turn around.

Rosie Charming, a friend of Aria's, is hurrying to catch up.

"Are you heading for the park?" she asks.

I wasn't, but it suddenly sounds like a great idea. The aunties would freak if they knew, but they're not my in loco parentises anymore. That makes me sadder than I thought it would.

"I was thinking of going to Starcups, but now that

you mention it, the park sounds like exactly where I need to be," I tell her. "I need a place to think."

"Cool," she says. "I'll walk with you. I'm going to the park to see Harold. He's an old friend of my parents who works there."

"What does he do?" I ask.

"These days he works for New York City Pest Control as a rat catcher," Rosie explains. "It's his retirement job, now that Mom and Dad are living in New York." She smiles. "Actually, if it weren't for Harold, I wouldn't be here. He was supposed to kill Mom, but he let her go."

"Hold on . . . do you mean Harold is *the* huntsman? The one who killed a deer and gave the queen its heart in a box instead?"

"Shhh! Don't say that so loud!" Rosie exclaims, looking over her shoulder. "I don't want to get him in trouble with the PETA folks."

"Sorry," I say. "But the reason he . . . well, you know what . . . was to save your mother's life. Doesn't that count for something?"

"You would think," Rosie says.

"So . . . there's actually a real-live huntsman . . . in Central Park," I say slowly.

Rosie laughs.

"He was definitely alive the last time I spoke to him," she says. "It going to be kind of an awkward visit if he's, *ya know*, dead."

"Great! That means I don't have to feel guilty about going to Central Park!"

Rosie gives me serious side-eye. "Why on earth would you feel guilty about going to the park? And what does Harold being alive have to do with it?" she asks. "Wait . . . do you suffer from musophobia?"

"I don't know," I confess. "What is it?"

"Rat phobia," Rosie says. "Or mouse phobia. Basically a fear of rodents."

"No. It's more like step-aunt phobia. You saw my aunties on Monday, right?"

Rosie giggles. "They were kind of hard to miss."

"Tell me about it," I say, realizing that, as embarrassed as I was by them on Monday, I will miss their unique brand of . . . eccentricity. "They wanted to walk me to school again the next day. When I said I wanted to go alone, they started telling me horror stories about Little Red Riding Hood and how she ended up in the bowels of the Big Bad Wolf. They warned me that if there hadn't been a handy-dandy huntsman in the vicinity to"—I lower my voice to a whisper in case any animal-rights people are around—"cut the wolf open and release Little Red Riding Hood and her grandma, they would have ended up as wolf poop."

Rosie gives me a quizzical look. "I'm still missing what this has to do with Harold."

I guess further explanation is necessary.

"The aunties didn't want me to go to Central Park due to the lack of lifesaving huntsmen," I explain. "Just in case there were any ravenous wolves around."

Rosie's lips twitch, and then she bursts out laughing. "And I thought *my* relatives were bizarre!" she says.

"At first I thought the aunties were embarrassingly weird. Then I got to know them better, and I've realized they're awesomely eccentric," I say. "But they have to leave and my parents might not let me ever see them again."

"Why?" she asks.

I fill her in on my sorry tale.

"And now my parents are coming home because they're convinced the aunties are a bad influence on me, and Eva's going to get away with stealing my shoe designs unless I can figure out a way to prove they're mine," I say. "And I have no idea what to do, which is why I need somewhere to think."

Rosie exhales loudly. "Wow. That's . . . a lot."

We arrive on the corner of Fifth Avenue and cross the street to the park. The trees are just starting to bud, bringing the hope of spring.

I could use some hope right about now.

"Well, here we are at the big bad park," Rosie says with a grin. "Are you scared yet?"

"Scared? Me?" I say. "The only things scaring me right now are that Eva's going to get away with it and that I won't see the aunties again."

"Well, I hope you figure it out," Rosie says. "I don't want Eva to win. It's not fair. Let me know if there's anything I can do."

"Thanks," I tell her. "That means a lot."

She stops as we reach a fork in the path. "Well, I have to go this way," she says, pointing with her thumb to the left. "If you head to the right, it'll take you to the lake. I find that's a good place to think."

"Then that's where I'll go," I say. "Give my regards to Harold, whose presence is making it possible for me to be here."

Rosie laughs and calls out, "Good luck! See you tomorrow!" as she takes the path to the south. I head to the lake and find an empty bench to sit on. The traffic noises are more faint in the middle of the park, and I can hear birds singing to one another in the nearby trees. If I close my eyes, I can almost pretend I'm back in Robicheaux.

But after a few minutes I open my eyes. Even though I miss Robicheaux, if we still lived there it would be even harder to be my own person. My last name is literally the name of the country because Dad's family has ruled there for centuries. Sure, that legacy has followed me here in the form of House of Robicheaux™ cleaning-products commercials, but still . . . I've got a better chance of becoming the Minty I want to be here in the Big Apple. If I can make it here, I can make it anywhere.

That's if I can figure out how to prove that Eva stole my ideas.

A little bird flutters over and sits on the arm of my bench. It cocks its head to the side, showing me the gold of its breast feathers, and it seems to be looking at me with its beady black eye.

"Got any suggestions?" I ask. "How can I prove that those designs were mine so I can go to the concert?"

The bird chirps a series of notes, hopping around excitedly. Then it flies off.

If only I spoke Bird . . .

A turtle is climbing out of the pond onto a flat rock at the water's edge. It moves slowly, but filled with determination, as it hauls its body up. It must be hard to carry your house around on your back all the time. It's bad enough carrying a backpack full of textbooks.

"Well, look who's here!"

I glance up and see Leila, the lady from the coffee shop. Today she's wearing a turquoise maxi dress, and her hair is tied up with a white scarf. She's carrying the same silver tote bag that she had when I met her in Starcups.

"Oh. Hi," I say.

"You look stressed again, Minty," she says. "What's on your mind?"

"I've got a problem I don't know how to solve," I say with a sigh.

"A problem shared is a problem halved," Leila says. "What's going on? Didn't you get your wish?"

"What wish?" I ask.

"You said you wanted to be known for something you did, rather than what your family did," she says. "Seems to me that's about to happen."

I stare at her, wondering if she's some kind of stalker. Maybe the aunties were wrong and encountering ravenous wolves isn't the biggest danger in Central Park.

"How do you know what's about to happen?" I ask, trying, unsuccessfully, to keep a wobble of fear out of my voice.

"Baby, don't you recognize your fairy godmother when you see her?" Leila says.

Not only is she a potential stalker, she's obviously been reading too many fairy tales.

"Uh, no. Mom wouldn't ever confirm or deny that the fairy-godmother tale was real," I say. "Or the bird-and-magic-tree one, either."

"Welcome to the life of a fairy godmother," Leila sighs. "I do all the work; then the person I did it for is all 'I built that!'"

She suddenly lets out a loud whistle, followed by a pattern of chirps. The next thing I know, a golden-breasted bird that looks exactly like the one that just flew away from the bench comes and sits on her shoulder, chirping loudly.

"I hear you, Goldenbreast. I'm sick of being underpaid and underappreciated too."

Okay, so she's a potential stalker who has read too many fairy tales and can talk to birds.

Meanwhile, I'm apparently losing my mind, because I'm starting to think that maybe she *is* my fairy godmother.

"So . . . if you are my fairy godmother, then how, exactly, is my wish coming true?"

She shakes her head. Goldenbreast the bird lets out a series of angry-sounding chirps. "You said you wanted to be known for something you did, not what your family did. When the police fine you for pulling the fire alarm and making your favorite band evacuate the hotel, it'll be all over the news and you'll be known, all right."

Her words hit me so hard, I lose my breath. "How . . . do . . . you . . . know?"

Leila glances sideways at the bird on her shoulder. "They're definitely slower to learn than they used to be," she says, shaking her head. Then, returning her gaze to me, she says, "I told you. I'm your fairy godmother. You told me your wish, and now it's going to come true."

"You really *are* my fairy godmother?" I gasp. "For *real*?"

"What, you expected an old white lady?" Leila says. "You kids are all brainwashed by that 'Bibbidi-Bobbidi-Boo' stuff—which they totally appropriated from *my* catchphrase spell, 'Hippity-Hoppity-Woo-Hoo!"

Why didn't Mom and Dad tell me any of this? Why am I the last to know everything?

"But . . . this isn't what I meant," I say, finally able to breathe properly again. "I want to be known for something *good*, not for getting into trouble."

Goldenbreast jumps off Leila's shoulder and flies around my head three times, chirping incessantly. Then he perches on the arm of the bench.

"I know, I know," Leila tells the bird. "How many times do we have to tell them to be specific when they make wishes? I've been in this business for two centuries and they never, ever learn."

Mom tells me to be careful what I wish for. Is she speaking from experience? Maybe there's more to the story than I've been told.

"But I didn't pull the fire alarm!" I exclaim. "I'm going to be known for something I didn't even do!"

The bird on Leila's shoulder looks at me, then turns to her and tilts its head to one side.

"Oops!" Leila says, avoiding my gaze. "Sorry, too late."

"Can I wish again?" I ask Leila. "To change the result of the first one? Especially since I didn't even know I was making a *wish* wish because you never told me you were my fairy godmother."

"My bad," she says. "But no can do. You've got to deal with the consequences of the first wish before you get a second one. The Fairy Godmother Guild is strict about the rules. I got a warning when I gave your mom those designer glass slippers."

"But what am I supposed to do?" I say, panic welling in my chest. "I'm only in middle school!"

"Have faith in yourself, Araminta of Robicheaux. You've got this."

"No . . . I don't! *I'm* the one who got myself into this mess in the first place!"

"Look around you," Leila says. "The answer is there if you're open to it."

A single tear slides down my cheek. I've been in New York for barely any time at all and I've already managed to mess up my life spectacularly.

"Oh, baby, don't cry on me," Leila says. She reaches out a finger and wipes the tear from my cheek. Then she snaps her fingers and there's a cup of steaming hot chocolate in her hand.

She hands it to me. "That'll help clear your head."

I take a sip, wondering if it's really hot chocolate or if it's some magic potion. It's creamy, chocolaty, and delicious, so I decide to drink it, even if I end up shrinking to grasshopper size like Alice in Wonderland.

Goldenbreast flies to Leila's shoulder and chirps.

"That's right, Goldie, we've got to go," Leila says. "So many wishes, so little time!"

And then they disappear: gone, as if they were never there.

I sit by the lake drinking the hot chocolate and feeling sorry for myself. Then I hear Leila's words in my head: *Have faith in yourself, Araminta of Robicheaux. You've got this.*

It remains to be seen if that's actually true, but if I ever want a chance for another wish (one that I will be sure to word very, very carefully), I have to try to solve the problems brought on by this one.

Dad tells me that he makes a pros-and-cons lists when he's trying to figure things out and make a decision. I pull out my social studies notebook and a pen. It's easier to start with the cons, because there are so many of them right now:

CONS
Eva stole my designs.
Eva has my notebook with the original
  sketches.
The police and Hotel Z think I pulled

the fire alarm and I could be in
serious trouble.

I can't make a new wish until I've
worked through the consequences of
the old one.

I might have messed up my parents'
quest for World Cleaning Product
Domination.

Because of me, Mom doesn't trust
the aunties anymore.

It's a pretty depressing list. I take another few sips of
hot chocolate and work on the things I have going for me:

PROS

I have the recording of Eva in the
bathroom admitting she put my
contest entries into a Hotel Z
envelope and pretended they were
hers—hypothetically at least.

I have the text convo where Eva
admitted she pulled the fire alarm.
Is that enough to get me out of
trouble???????

> Livvy said I'm much better at
> sketching than Eva.
> I have friends who want to help me
> prove that I really won the contest.

I chew on the end of my pen until I realize the most important thing of all:

> I know I designed the winning
> shoes and I could draw them
> again if I wanted to. Could
> Eva??????????????????????

I stare at the list and sip Leila's cup of tear-generated hot chocolate until it's empty. That's when I realize what I have to do, even if it means that I'll never escape my family legacy.

Chapter Eleven

I EXIT CENTRAL PARK, HAVING MANAGED TO
survive without the services of Harold the Huntsman,
and text the aunties.

> Me: Are you still there? I need to talk to you DESPERATELY
>
> AuntieL: Are we still where?
>
> AuntieM: She means here, duh!
>
> AuntieL: Here where?

I have to stop this before they start fighting.

> Me: At my apartment. Well, technically my parents'
> apartment, but I live there too.
>
> AuntieL: Oh! Yes we're still there. Or is it here?
>
> AuntieM: How are we even related, let alone twins?!!!!

Me: I'm on my way home—PLEASE DON'T LEAVE YET!

AuntieL: But Ella said she wants us out.

Me: I need you! Please stay!

AuntieM: She needs us, Lottie.

AuntieM: They'll have to drag us out of here, Minty.

Me: xoxox See you soon!

I check my watch. It's already four o'clock. My parents' flight lands in an hour, and they want the aunties gone by the time they get back. I run the last eight blocks to the apartment and arrive sweating and panting, with a painful stitch in my side.

When Aunt Lottie sees me walk in the door clutching my diaphragm, my face as hot and red as a chili pepper, she immediately assumes the worst.

"MARGE! Call 911! Minty is dying!"

"I'm . . . not . . . dying . . . ," I pant. "I . . . just . . . ran . . . home."

"Oh," Aunt Lottie says. "MARGE! Ix-nay on the iying-day!"

"Huh?" I manage to wheeze out before dropping my backpack in the middle of the living room floor and collapsing onto the sofa.

"Pig latin," Aunt Lottie says, like that's supposed to

mean something to me. "MARGE! Et-gay oor-yay utt-bay in-way ere-hay!"

"Is Minty dying or not?" Aunt Margaux says as she comes into the living room. Apparently she doesn't see the backpack I dropped on the floor, because she trips over it, pinwheels, and lands on the armchair . . . which also happens to be where Aunt Lottie is sitting.

"I'm not," I say, my breath gradually beginning to recover.

"She isn't, Marge, but are you trying to kill *me*?" Aunt Lottie groans, pushing her sister off.

"Someone's trying to kill *me* by leaving things to trip over in the middle of the floor!" Aunt Margaux says, standing up and pointing to the offending backpack. "And stop calling me Marge!"

"No one is trying to kill anyone!" I say, hoping to end another auntie argument before it starts. "But Eva Murgatroyd stole my shoe designs and won the VIP tickets to the Retro of Sync concert!"

This has the desired effect on Aunt Margaux.

"She *what*?" Aunt Margaux shouts.

"You design shoes?" Aunt Lottie says, a huge smile breaking across her face.

"Wait . . . *that* was the contest? To design *footwear*?" Aunt Margaux says.

I nod, trying to hide the mixed emotions I feel about the aunties discovering my secret passion for shoe design. But while I was living dangerously in Central Park, I realized that if I don't want Eva to get away with what she did, I might have to give up that secret in return for their help. If it's a choice between being known as the aunties' niece who designs shoes or Eva Murgatroyd's fall girl, I'll take the aunties in a heartbeat.

"That Eva has committed a double crime," Aunt Lottie says. "She stole designs, and she won the contest by lying."

"A triple crime—she messed with *our niece*," Aunt Margaux says.

"A quadruple crime—she *purposely* made me her fall girl," I add.

"Are we going to let her get away with this?" Aunt Lottie asks.

"*Ix-nay on the et-gay way-agay ith-way it-way!*" Aunt Margaux shouts.

I'm not sure what she just said, but I'm pretty sure it means no. It makes me feel so much better to know the aunties are on my side.

"How are we going to prove this?" Aunt Lottie says.

"I've got a recording of her admitting what she did, except it was like, 'Hypothetically, if I did do it, this is what I did,'" I say. "But Livvy has a text where Eva admits she made me the fall girl."

"And Marge has that screenshot where she admitted she pulled the fire alarm," Aunt Lottie says.

"It's Margaux!" my other aunt shouts. One auntie is clearly on her last nerve with the other one, but the clock is ticking, so I can't afford for them to fight.

"I have an idea, but I need your help," I say, hoping to keep them on task—namely, saving me from big trouble and Eva from getting away with stealing my designs.

"Minty needs our help, Marge!" Aunt Lottie says, clapping her hands excitedly.

I take it as a sign of the depth of Aunt Margaux's love for me that she bites back another reminder not to call her that and instead asks: "Tell us your idea, Minty. What can we do?"

"I realized that since Eva stole my sketchbook, I don't have the proof that they're my designs," I say. "But then I remembered something Livvy said. Eva can't draw anywhere as well as me. So I was thinking: if there's any way we can get the Retro of Sync people to listen, maybe we could settle it with a draw-off."

"A draw-off?" Aunt Lottie says, rubbing her chin. "You mean like you both have to draw a shoe design on the spot, in front of an audience?"

"Yes," I say.

"I like it . . . ," Aunt Margaux says slowly. "It would be even better with cameras there. . . ."

"She might not have our blood, but she's definitely our niece," Aunt Lottie says, beaming with pride. "It's a cunning plan."

"It is," Aunt Margaux agrees. "And the potential marketing opportunities are endless. . . . Send me that recording, right away." She whips out her cell and starts striding out of the room. "Leave everything to me, Minty."

Before I really got to know the aunties, that idea would have filled me with dread. But now it feels like a huge weight has been lifted, because the aunties are on the case.

That's when I get a text from Mom.

Landed safely. We'll be home soon. WE NEED TO HAVE A SERIOUS TALK.

Ugh—Mom talking about having a "serious talk" in all caps never bodes well.

Now I just have to figure out how to deal with my parents.

✦

Aunt Margaux is still in her room working the phones and I'm with Aunt Lottie in the kitchen preparing a peace-offering dinner for my parents when Mom and Dad walk in the front door.

"Minty! We're home!" Dad calls out. "Something smells delicious."

I race out to greet them before they realize the aunties haven't vacated the premises.

"Greetings, beloved parents," I say. "I've missed you *so much*!"

Mom and Dad exchange a worried glance.

"She must be in much worse trouble than we thought," Mom says.

Dad nods. "Is that Margaux's voice I hear?"

"Yes, but—"

"What are they still doing in this apartment?" Mom asks. "I said I wanted them gone by the time we arrived home."

"I know, but—"

"I should have known better than to leave you with them." Mom shakes her head. "I really thought they'd changed. I'm such a sucker; I never should have—"

"MOM, LISTEN TO ME!" I shout in frustration.

"They *have* changed. They're still here because I asked them for their help!"

"Ella, it sounds like this is going to be quite the tale. Let's take a load off our feet while we hear it," Dad says. "It's been a long day."

"And it's about to get even worse," Mom mutters, but she heads into the kitchen and we follow her.

"Ella! Robbie! Welcome home," Aunt Lottie says, her voice more high-pitched than usual and a nervous smile on her face. "We've got mutton stew, roasted potatoes, and honeyed carrots for dinner."

"My favorite," Dad says.

"And almond apple tart for dessert," Aunt Lottie continues.

"Ella's favorite," Dad says.

"Robbie, you know this is because they're trying to butter us up so we'll forget that we had to cut our trip short because, thanks to them, Minty is in trouble with the police, right?" Mom says.

"Mom, it wasn't their fault," I say. "Take a seat so I can tell you how it all *really* went down."

Mom exhales as she and Dad sit at the kitchen table. Aunt Lottie brings them each a cup of tea. "You must be tired after such a long trip," she says.

"Thank you, Lottie," Mom says. "We are. Especially since we had to cancel important business meetings to come home."

Aunt Lottie bites her lip. "We're sorry," she says. "Please—"

"Let's hear Minty's explanation first," Dad says, cutting her off.

So I launch into my whole sad tale. As I tell it, I watch my parents carefully to see if they believe me, but they've both got their poker faces on. It's a skill they probably learned from their business negotiations for House of Robicheaux™.

"I was stupid to believe Eva, but I wanted to go to the concert so badly," I say. "Retro of Sync has never toured in Robicheaux. Never ever."

"I suppose doing an obvious thing like asking us to buy tickets was out of the question?" Dad asks.

"It was sold out!" I protest. "The only way to get tickets was to win the contest, and I found out about that the day after entries closed. So I had to figure out another way to get my entries to the band, and Eva had a solution." I sigh heavily. "Or so I thought . . ."

"This Eva girl is bad news," Aunt Lottie says. "She keeps calling and e-mailing Comfortably Ever After asking for free shoes because she's a 'social-media influencer.'"

"And her parents are crazy rich, so she could totally afford to buy them," I say.

"Hold on . . . what's her last name again?" Dad asks.

"Murgatroyd," I tell him.

"Is she Don Murgatroyd's daughter?" Mom says. "That would explain a lot."

"What do you mean?" I ask.

"Don Murgatroyd is the chairman of Malvado Corporation," Dad explains. "They tried to bribe one of our managers to give them the formula for the Crud Crusher, but fortunately, he told us instead of selling it to Murgatroyd."

"It pays to reward honesty," Mom says.

"Mr. Murgatroyd got us the internship at the Hotel Z," I say. "He knows the owner."

"Hmmm," Mom says, tapping her finger on the side of her teacup. "No wonder they're not looking into Eva for pulling the fire alarm."

"It sounds like the apple didn't fall far from the tree," Aunt Lottie says.

"Just like your little Minty apple," Aunt Margaux says, coming into the kitchen and putting her arm around me. "She's just as great a fruit as you are, Ella."

Then, looking at Dad, she says, "Well, and you, too, Robbie."

"I think I'm flattered," Dad says. "That was a compliment, right?"

"Oh yes!" Aunt Lottie says, nodding vigorously. "We love our little Minty apple."

Mom still isn't quite ready to forgive the aunties yet, though.

"My father never got a call from the police about me," she says.

"Fact-check: not true," Aunt Margaux says.

"That's right!" Aunt Lottie says, slapping her forehead. "How could I have forgotten? The cemetery keeper called the police when he saw you running out of there in the silver-and-gold ball gown Goldenbreast gave you, because he thought you were a grave robber!"

"We had such a chuckle with Mother about that," Aunt Margaux.

"Wait—so Leila really *was* your fairy godmother, and Goldenbreast was the bird in the tale?"

"Yes to both counts," Mom says. "And I only got the

dress and the glass slippers so I could meet Dad after making a few wish mistakes of my own!"

I'm stunned into silence.

"The first time, I mumbled about wishing to go to the ball, and she misheard the wish and turned me into a beach ball!" Mom laughs. "Let me tell you, it was really hard figuring out how to reverse that one!"

"And then the second time, Mom said she wished she could meet the prince, but she didn't specify which one, so Leila sent my cousin Frank to the village market to meet her," Dad says. "Frank's a great guy, but . . ."

"He doesn't hold a candle to your father in the looks department," Mom says. "Leila made me get myself out of the trouble those first wishes got me into before she'd grant the one I actually meant. Getting the wish you want is never as easy as they make it sound in the tales."

"And it's not always a handsome prince who swoops in to save the day," Dad adds. "I was merely the icing on the cake after Mom worked things out for herself."

"My absolute favorite icing," Mom says, glancing over at Dad lovingly. "On the very best cake."

"Ugh," I say. "Can we not get all mushy, please?"

"We'll refrain from 'mushiness' as long as you promise that if Leila ever offers you another wish, you'll be *very* specific," Mom says.

"I promise," I tell her. "In my own defense, I didn't know that I was talking to my fairy godmother when I made the first wish."

Dad chuckles. "That Leila sure is something," he says, shaking his head.

I don't find the situation at all chuckle-worthy right now. "Can we get back to stopping Eva from getting away with stealing my designs?"

"Have no fear, Minty, your aunties are here," Margaux says, walking into the room. "And everything is going to plan."

"That doesn't fill me with confidence," Mom says. "Not after having to take the first plane home from Paris."

I would have said the same thing when the aunties arrived on Sunday. But I know my aunts really *have* changed, just like Mom told me before she left. It's strange how our roles have reversed.

Ignoring Mom's dig, Aunt Margaux tells us what she's been working on.

"I got in touch with the Retro of Sync people and told them Eva won the contest under false pretenses. I also sent them the recording you got of Eva confessing, at least hypothetically. And the screenshot of the texts."

"What happened?" I ask, starting to feel a smidgen of hope.

"They agreed there was enough to investigate, so they confronted the Murgatroyds with the evidence," Aunt Margaux says. "Of course Eva denied it. Don Murgatroyd threatened to sue you for libel and for taking an unauthorized recording in a bathroom. He also said he would sue the band for breach of contract."

"I'm only thirteen!" I protest. "Am I old enough to be sued for libel?"

"Don't worry—Aunt Margaux is way ahead of you," she says. "I'd already texted the police the screenshot of Eva confessing that she pulled the fire alarm, and they called the Murgatroyds on one of their other lines while I was on the phone with Don. Meanwhile, I threatened to countersue unless they agreed to settle the matter with a public draw-off."

"What did they say?" Aunt Lottie asks, clasping her hand to her chest.

"They agreed!" Aunt Margaux says, with a triumphant smile. "Tomorrow, in your school gym, at eleven o'clock. I had to make another big donation to your school, this time to the PTA, before Mr. Hamilton would agree to open the building on a Saturday. The band will be there to judge, and they're going to stream it live on their fan site." She winks at me. "A little bird might have alerted the local news stations about these developments too."

"Do you mean Theo Downey and Retro of Sync *are coming to my school*?" I screech.

"Isn't that what I just said?" Aunt Margaux says. "You need to use some of that Crud Crusher stuff in your ears."

"Ooh! I'm so excited to meet Theo Downer!" Aunt Lottie exclaims.

I fling my arms around my aunt. "Aunt Margaux, you're the best!" Then, wanting to ensure there isn't any intersibling fighting, I hug my other aunt and say, "You too, Aunt Lottie!"

Then I glance over at my parents. "Please can they stay?" I beg them. "None of this was their fault."

"Well, except for Marge nearly setting fire to the kitchen when she tried to make lamb chops," Aunt Lottie says.

"Stop exaggerating!" Aunt Margaux says. "And my name isn't Marge, for the gazillionth time."

"Gazillionth? Now who is exaggerating?" Lottie retorts.

Dad and Mom exchange a loaded glance, but I'm not sure what exactly it means.

"Time out!" Mom says, finally. "And yes, they can stay."

My aunties' smiles are so big I worry that their faces will crack in two.

"As long as you stop fighting," Dad adds.

Like *that's* ever going to happen. I don't think Lottie and Margaux could survive an hour without getting into an argument of some kind. It's who they are.

"How about we eat this dinner Minty and I made to celebrate?" Lottie says. "I can hear Robbie's stomach growling from here."

Dad looks down at his stomach. "That sounds like a capital idea, Lottie."

As I help Aunt Lottie serve the stew, I wonder if asking my aunts for help counts as working through the consequences of my first wish. Even if it doesn't, I've got another chance to prove myself, thanks to Aunt Margaux.

"This is really delicious, Lottie," Dad says after tasting the stew.

"When did you learn to cook?" Mom asks. "The only time I remember seeing you two in the kitchen was when you were throwing peas and lentils into the hearth ashes for me to pick out."

Both aunties look shamefaced.

"We were so horrible to you," Margaux says. "What was the matter with us, Lottie?"

"I know it was because Hortensia encouraged you," Mom says.

"Mother is one of the reasons I learned to cook. I took it up as soon as we got away from her. She was the one who gave us the idea to cut things off so the shoe fit," Aunt Lottie says, her voice taking on a bitter tone. "She handed us a knife and said, 'Once you become queen, you won't have to walk anymore.'"

"Wow," I say. "That's . . . brutal."

"Our mother was very ambitious," Aunt Margaux says. She sounds more sad than bitter. "She wanted us to climb the social ladder—but the only way she could see us doing that was by *marrying* someone rich and powerful. She never had the confidence that we could become rich and powerful by ourselves."

"I often wonder what she would think about our success with Comfortably Ever After," Aunt Lottie says. "When we told her we'd won our first contract, she didn't even congratulate us. All she wanted to know was: 'Are you dating anyone? So when are you going to get married?'"

"It was a different time," Dad says.

The aunties look at each other and burst out laughing.

"Oh, Robbie, you really think so?" Aunt Margaux says. "That's so cute."

I hope Dad's right and the aunties are wrong. But just in case, I'm going to make sure to learn everything I can from Margaux and Lottie, so that I don't end up doing something desperate like cutting my toes or heel off to "win" a prince. I'm determined to make it on my own.

After dinner I practice sketching the competition designs in preparation for the draw-off. As soon as I finish one sketch, the aunties practically rip it out of my hands and make comments.

"Ooh, I love this one," Aunt Lottie says. "You've got a real talent for this, Minty!"

Aunt Margaux spreads the various sketches on the coffee table and examines them thoughtfully.

"Do you think the youths would wear Comfortably Ever After shoes if they looked like this?" she says.

"Can I be honest?" I ask.

"No, please lie." Aunt Margaux rolls her eyes. "Of course we want you to be honest!"

"Your shoes are amazingly comfortable, but . . . well . . . they're kind of ugly. I was trying to design shoes as comfortable as yours, but more . . . fashionable."

"Marge, are you thinking what I'm thinking?" Aunt Lottie asks.

"I'm not a mind reader, Lottie, but I think I might be."

"What are you thinking?" I ask.

"If we tell you, it won't be a surprise," Aunt Lottie says.

I don't know if I should be excited or concerned. I'm not sure I can handle any more surprises right now.

At three o'clock in the morning, I wake up in a cold sweat. I'd been dreaming that Mom died in a plane crash and Dad remarried a lady who turned me into an unpaid servant. My dream stepmother handed me a kitchen knife and ordered me to cut off my toes so they could fit into a pair of hideously ugly Comfortably Ever After™ shoes, and then she made me dance in them with a prince who looked like Dakota. Her daughters were laughing at me as we danced, because I couldn't remember the right moves and I kept stepping on Dakota's toes. The scariest part of all—both daughters had Eva's face.

Chapter Twelve

MY HEAD FEELS HEAVY WHEN I WAKE UP, and my stomach churns with a mixture of fear and anticipation. What if Eva can draw better than Livvy led me to believe? What if she practiced really hard to copy my designs? After all, she has my sketchbook to work from, and I just have my brain. Given what a mess I've made of things lately, I'm not sure if that's going to be enough. To top it off, an enormous zit has emerged on my chin overnight.

I find Mom sitting at the kitchen table, sipping coffee from her Dirt Destroyer™ mug.

"Been up since four," she says. "Jet lag. Can I make you some breakfast?"

"I'm too nervous to be hungry."

"Never face a hard day without a good breakfast," Mom tells me, just like the aunties said.

"Fine. I'll get a granola bar."

Mom has her head in her hands when I sit down at the table. I don't know if it's because she's so tired, or because of . . . me.

"I'm sorry you had to come home," I tell her. "Is everything going to be okay with the global expansion, despite having to cut the trip short?"

She lifts her head, drinks some more coffee, and then puts the mug on the table with a deliberateness that makes me wonder if she's figuring out what to say. "I think so. We'd already signed one contract, but we had to cancel a big meeting yesterday."

I see her furrowed brow and the dark circles under her eyes and feel even worse.

"I'm sorry I messed things up for you."

"We all make mistakes," Mom says with a sigh. "It was probably a mistake to go on this trip so soon after uprooting you from Robicheaux. But we were excited to have this opportunity to grow the business." She covers my hand with hers, which is nice and warm from her coffee mug. "Maybe we lost track of what was really important—you."

"I *was* upset at first," I admit. "But now I'm glad you went, because it gave me a chance to get to know the aunties. They're actually pretty cool."

"They are," Mom says, her lips quirked into a half smile. "A little wacky, but definitely cool."

"What happens if Eva wins and gets away with stealing my designs? It would be so unfair."

"Life's not always fair, Minty," Mom says gently. "Do you think it was fair that my father let Hortensia turn me into an unpaid servant after Mother died?"

"No way!" I say. "Why did he?"

It's as if a cloud of sadness descends over my mom, and I wish I hadn't asked the question. But I need to know. My parents focus on the romantic part of their tale, like how Dad was so taken with Mom's beauty that he became lovesick at the thought of not being able to marry her. Mom doesn't like to talk about the stuff that came before it all that much—well, except when she wants to tell me how spoiled I am because my life is so much easier than hers was.

"My father was . . . well, after Mother died, he was so overcome with grief that he couldn't imagine being able to raise me. Hortensia saw a helpless, grieving widower and . . . persuaded him that he needed her to carry on," Mom says. "He was so grateful to her for taking over the household that he didn't question anything she did."

"But . . . didn't he realize she was treating you badly?"

Mom wraps both of her hands around her coffee cup, as if the memory chills her and she needs to absorb the warmth.

"Hortensia tried to make sure I didn't get a chance to speak to him alone," she says, looking down at her hands. "One day I managed to see him for a few minutes, and I complained about how my stepmother and her daughters were treating me." She looks up at me. "When he took it up with Hortensia, she told him that teenage girls are 'known to be prone to exaggeration and hysteria.'"

"Wow. That's so wrong," I say. "And your father believed her?"

Mom nods. "I learned that teenage girls aren't believed all too often." She gets up and pours herself some more coffee. "But that made me more determined to make my voice heard, loud and strong, so that you wouldn't have to grow up that way."

She sits back down. "You'll always face challenges in your life, Minty. The thing that makes the difference is how you learn from them." She smiles at me. "In the meantime, just fake it till you make it."

"I've learned that I shouldn't trust people when my gut tells me not to, even if I really want something," I say.

"Good lesson," says Aunt Lottie as she walks into the kitchen. "You've got this, Minty."

I really hope she's right.

Images of shoes swim around my brain as we all walk to Manhattan World Themes for the draw-off. A taxi almost hits me when I'm crossing Third Avenue because I'm so busy drawing designs in my head. Then I see the advertisement for the Retro of Sync concert on a passing bus, and it hits me that Theo Downey is going to be at my school watching me sketch in, like, an hour. Not only that, but the draw-off is going to be streamed to who knows how many people as it happens.

My stomach churns at the thought.

There's a crowd of students outside school—not as many as on a weekday, but a surprising number for a weekend.

"Minty!" Nina calls out, and I see Dakota standing

next to her. The last thing I want is for my parents to meet him.

"I'll be back in a minute," I say to my parents and the aunties. "Wait here."

"What are you guys doing here?" I ask. "For that matter, what are all these people doing here?"

"Isn't there supposed to be some kind of draw-off between you and Eva today?" Dakota asks.

"And isn't Retro of Sync going to be there to judge it?" Nina adds.

"Wow, news travels fast," I say.

Dakota gives me a quizzical look. "Eva is involved," he says. "She's taking all the credit for the fact that THEO DOWNEY"—he says that in a very loud falsetto—"is going to grace our school with his presence!"

"You're just jealous," Nina says, poking his arm. "Because Minty thinks Theo is adorable."

I'm not sure whose face turns pinker when she says that, Dakota's or mine. I'm not about to tell them that I think Dakota is pretty cute too.

"I don't want Eva to get away with stealing Minty's shoe designs," Dakota says. "If it means THEO DOWNEY has to come and judge the draw-off, I'm okay with that." He grins. "I'm just glad I have my headphones so I don't get deafened by all the screaming when he walks into the auditorium."

"I'm sorry I didn't listen to you when you tried to warn me about Eva," I confess. "I shouldn't have believed a word she said."

"Why did you?" Dakota asks. "Listen to Eva instead of us, that is."

"I thought her plan was my only chance to win tickets for Retro of Sync," I tell him. "I mean, it did get my designs in front of Theo Downey after the competition closed, and the band chose them as the winner."

"Yeah, except Eva said they were hers," Nina says. "We warned you."

"Eva's . . . well, let's just say she wasn't that nice to us when we first moved here," Dakota adds.

"She called Dakota a hayseed, and me a country bumpkin," Nina says.

"She only talked to me after the aunties filmed the commercial," I admit. "I should have known better. But I'd just moved here, and my parents had jetted off to Europe to achieve World Cleaning Product Domination."

"Well, at least you know who your real friends are now. Right, Dakota?"

Her brother nods, meeting my gaze. "We're here for you, Minty. If you want us, that is."

"You guys," I say, feeling my eyes start to get warm and prickly.

My life in New York City is definitely looking up, even if I don't win the draw-off. But still—I *really* hope I do.

As I walk back to my family, other students ask me about the Retro of Sync visit.

"Hey, Minty, good luck," Rosie Charming's friend Nicole says.

"I can't believe *Theo Downey* is coming to Manhattan World Themes!" her friend Katie says, in a voice that sounds so uncannily like Dakota's falsetto that I have to swallow a snort of laughter as I glance over at him. He gives me an adorable half grin that makes my toes curl in my black platform boots.

The more people talk about the draw-off, the more nervous I get. *What if I mess up? What if Eva wins?*

I'll have to transfer to another school. How would I ever be able to show my face at MWTMS if I lost a draw-off of my own designs?

"Let's go inside," I tell my parents and the aunties. "I'm starting to freak out."

Mom and Dad each take one of my hands, and together we walk into the building, flanked by the aunties, who of course start fighting with each other about who should go first when we can't all fit through the door at the same time.

Principal Hamilton comes rushing over as soon as he spots me in the school lobby. He looks almost as frazzled as I feel.

"Things certainly have been very . . . *lively* . . . since you arrived at Manhattan World Themes Middle School, Araminta," he says, taking a tissue out of the pocket of his khakis and wiping his forehead. "I hope it won't always be like this."

"I promise you it was totally boring at my old school," I tell him. "It must be New York City."

"Just think about all the enrichment programs you can pay for thanks to Minty's . . . *liveliness*," Aunt Margaux says.

"Yes, quite," Mr. Hamilton says. "Well, I better go make sure that everything's going smoothly."

We follow him into the auditorium. There are two easels set up on stage, each with a camera tripod behind it. Several other camera people are wafting around the front stage area, as a guy with an Australian accent gives directions on how the live stream will be shot.

I sit with family, getting more nervous by the second as the auditorium slowly fills up.

The Australian director, whose name is Barry, calls Eva and me onstage and assigns us each an easel.

"There will be a camera on each of you for close-ups," he warns us. "So don't pick your nose unless you want all the Syncos to see it."

He gets a text and looks down at his phone. "Retro of Sync is in the building," he announces to the assembled crowd. People start clapping and *woo-hoo*ing.

Theo Downey is the first one to enter the auditorium. He's wearing skinny-leg black jeans, a T-shirt that says SYNC OR SWIM, a leather jacket, and dark sunglasses, even though he's inside.

The screams prompted by his appearance reverberate off the walls. But screams aren't the only thing accompanying Theo Downey and the other band members. Two big bodyguards in black suits precede them, and two even bigger ones follow them into the auditorium. Still, the band members stop and take selfies with kids on the aisle, until a bodyguard points to his watch and then the stage.

I stand next to my easel, trying to avoid looking over at Eva and her dad, who walked in with his own entourage right before the band arrived and is sitting in the front row on her side of the stage. Instead I focus on my parents and the aunties, who are in the front row on my side, and my friends, who are sitting right behind them.

You're in it to win it! I keep telling myself.

At 10:55, Mr. Hamilton comes to center stage and tries to get everyone to be quiet. "I want to see your best MWTMS behavior, because in five minutes' time, this live stream is going out to thousands of people."

"More like millions," Theo says.

Nothing like knowing how many people could see you make a fool of yourself to make you feel like you're going to projectile-vomit in front of your peers—and a million others watching around the world.

Then I see Aunt Lottie and Dad giving me frantic thumbs-ups, and Aunt Margaux doing a heart sign with her hands, and Mom mouthing, *I love you—you've got this.* Behind them my friends are all giving me looks and gestures of encouragement too. I glance down at my hands and hope they stop trembling so I can draw.

Mr. Hamilton introduces the members of the band, like we don't already know who they are. They're famous!

"Welcome to Manhattan World Themes Middle School, Retro of Sync. I'm sorry your visit isn't under more pleasant circumstances."

"We're one minute to live stream," Australia Man warns. Mr. Hamilton goes backstage and Australia Man counts down, "Live in five, four, three, two, one . . ."

"*Helloooooo*, Manhattan World Themes Middle School!" Theo says. Cue more cheering and screaming. If my eardrums survive this draw-off intact, it will be a miracle. "Why am I losing my precious beauty sleep to be in a school when I didn't do very well there the first time around?"

"You're gorgeous anyway, Theo!" someone shouts out.

"Thank you, darling," Theo says. "Now, the reason we're here is because it seems there's been a bit of controversy about the winning entry of our competition."

The camera on Eva's side of the stage moves in tight to her easel.

"Yesterday we announced that the winner of the VIP experience for Saturday night's show was Eva Murgatroyd," Theo says.

Eva smiles into the camera, looking as cool as a cucumber, like she isn't a lying, cheating, shoe-design stealer.

"But then our PR people got a phone call claiming that Eva Murgatroyd didn't actually sketch the winning designs," Theo continues. "The caller maintained that the *real* winner should have been Araminta Robicheaux."

The camera closest to me zooms in, and I try to smile like I'm not scared witless and worried about the enormous zit that feels like it's growing exponentially while my face is being live-streamed to a gazillion people.

"And that, my dearest Syncos, is why I'm awake before noon when we're performing tonight, and I'm standing on the stage of a New York City middle school," Theo says. "Because we're going to settle this with a draw-off."

The screaming and cheering that erupts makes my head spin. Will I faint, puke, or burst a zit first?

In it to win it. In it to win it, I repeat to myself, trying to stay upright and puke-free. I've given up on being able to control my zit.

"Our head bodyguard, Ray, has the original entry in that swanky black briefcase he's carrying," Theo continues. "Both of the alleged shoe designers will have ten minutes to sketch the designs as they remember them; then we'll judge who the real contest winner should be."

"You'll be able to vote too," says Tom Donham, the ROS drummer. "You'll find a link to the poll in the lower right corner of the live stream. "So be sure to cast your vote for either Eva or Araminta."

"Okay, who has the stopwatch?" Theo asks.

"That would be me," Jimmy Strage, the lead guitarist says. He pulls a stopwatch out of the pocket of his leather jacket. "Ladies, pick up your pencils."

At least Snowball didn't poop on his *jacket,* I think as I pick up the pencil and take a deep breath to try to calm my trembling fingers.

"You have ten minutes to sketch at least one of the designs you submitted to the contest. On your marks . . . get set . . . *draw*!" Jimmy says.

As soon as I hear the word "draw," I start sketching furiously from memory. If Eva hadn't stolen my sketchbook, I'd be more confident. But if she hadn't stolen it, I would have had it as proof that I did the designs, and we wouldn't be doing a draw-off in front of . . . *OMG,* do not *think about how many people are watching right now!*

When the timer goes off and Theo shouts, "Girls, step back from your easels and drop your pencils!" I hope that I've remembered well enough to prove that the design was mine.

"Can we turn the easels to the front of the stage?" Theo says. "Tommy, what about a drumroll?"

Tom pulls a pair of drumsticks out of his back pocket and does a roll on the podium as two ROS roadies slowly rotate our easels to the front of the stage. Even though he's a pretty great drummer, my heart is beating way faster than his sticks.

Then I see what Eva has drawn, and my heart almost stops, because hers looks almost identical to the design I did from memory. She must have practiced copying the designs in my sketchbook last night, while I've had to draw 100 percent from recollection.

"Well, isn't this interesting?" Theo says. He calls over the bodyguard with the briefcase and opens it. Withdrawing a piece of paper, he holds it up to the nearest camera and then turns it to the audience.

"Both contestants drew one of the entries—the design for my shoes, which, I have to say, is absolutely brilliant," Theo says.

Despite the fact that I feel sick to my stomach thinking Eva might get away with this, I can't help breaking into a huge grin, because *Theo Downey thinks I'm brilliant!* At least he thinks my shoe design is, anyway.

"It's impossible to tell who designed it from this competition," bassist Chad Apollo says.

I hear boos from the audience, but they sound like

they're coming from the other end of a very long tunnel. I can't believe this is happening.

"Eva stole Minty's sketchbook!" Aunt Margaux's voice rings out loud and clear over the general hubbub in the auditorium.

"Did I hear someone say that Eva stole Minty's sketchbook?" Theo asks. He looks over at me. "I presume Minty is you, Araminta?"

I don't trust myself to speak, so I just nod.

"That would add a new wrinkle, wouldn't it?" Chad says.

"I didn't steal it!" Eva shouts, but she won't look in my direction, because she knows she's lying.

"I'm going to sue you for libel!" Mr. Murgatroyd shouts across the auditorium at Aunt Margaux.

"It's not libel if it's true!" Aunt Margaux retorts. "I checked with my lawyer."

Theo and the rest of the band look like they're watching a tennis match; their heads swivel from one side of the auditorium to the other as my auntie gets into it with Eva's dad.

Finally, Mr. Hamilton comes out from the wings and shouts: "Okay, TIME OUT!"

Mr. Murgatroyd starts to argue with him, but Mr.

Hamilton isn't having any of it, despite the warning call he got from the chancellor this morning.

"Sir, I'm asking you to think about the example you're setting for the students of Manhattan World Themes Middle School," he tells Mr. Murgatroyd. "We strive to encourage a community where students can resolve conflicts without resorting to threats." He glares down at Mr. Murgatroyd. "Threats of *any* kind."

Ooooh, burn!

"Mr. Hamilton, do you have any suggestions for how to solve this?" Theo asks.

Our principal gazes at the two almost identical drawings.

"Well . . . it's certainly strange that both Minty and Eva drew the same design," he says. "But if Eva did steal Minty's sketchbook, she would have had time to practice copying it." He strokes his beard, deep in thought. "Meanwhile, how would Minty have known what to draw if she hadn't done the original design?"

"Good point," Theo says.

"But what if Eva did the design and Minty sketched her own version in her book?" Mr. Hamilton continues.

"Hey, man, I thought you were going to help clear things up," Chad says.

"Yeah, you're just making it all murkier, if you ask me," Tom adds.

"Sorry—I'm thinking this through aloud so our students see how adults problem-solve." He glares in Mr. Murgatroyd's direction. "*Without* resorting to threats."

"Let us know when you get to the suggestion part," Theo says. "We've only got the sound check for a show at a major New York arena tonight."

Mr. Hamilton's face flushes. "Yes, well . . . here's my idea. What if we set the girls a *new* design task that they have to do right here, right now? That will give us more data to make a decision."

The band members look from one to another, and apparently it's some kind of wordless communication, because Theo says, "Yeah . . . we like it."

They huddle up and move away from the mic. When they break apart, Theo comes back to the mic and says, "Okay. Our viewers here and around the world . . . we've decided on the tiebreaker challenge."

Tom Donham does another drumroll.

"Eva and Minty: Your mission, if you choose to accept it, is . . ." He pauses for dramatic effect. "Design a shoe that best expresses the new single from our latest album: 'A Million Miles to the Nearest Star.'"

"You have ten minutes to sketch your design," Jimmy Strage says, looking at the stopwatch. "On your marks . . . get set . . . draw!"

I take a few seconds to think about the chorus lyrics, singing them under my breath as I try to figure out how I can express them in a shoe that's comfortable and looks good.

> *I love you for who you are.*
> *I'll follow you baby*
> *Even minus a car.*
> *It doesn't matter*
> *How near or how far.*
> *A million miles*
> *To the nearest star.*

Judging by the shout of "Go, Eva, you're gonna win this!" it sounds like she's already started. I keep my eyes closed and try to block out the noise, sketching the design in my head before I put anything on paper, just like I always do.

A star. Two rocket ships, the one with the boy following the one with the girl, shown on opposite sides of each shoe. Two hearts: one whole and one broken, just like mine will be if Eva wins.

Taking a deep breath, I open my eyes and start to draw the design I've got in my head. I barely hear the noise in the auditorium as I sketch with intense focus, transferring my ideas to the page.

I lose track of time, just like I always do when I draw. It's not till I hear Jimmy saying "two more minutes" that I realize eight minutes have already passed. Luckily, my sketch is pretty fleshed out; both the right and left shoes are complete, so I use the last two minutes to embellish the basic design even further.

"Ten . . . nine . . . eight . . . seven . . . six . . . five . . . four . . . three . . . two . . . *one*! Time's up!" Chad shouts.

I step back from the easel and look at my sketch. I'm proud of what I've done. When I look into the audience, I see Mom and Dad smiling encouragingly as the aunties beam and give me thumbs-ups. My friends in the row behind are all making hearts with their fingers. I do it right back. I just hope their confidence in me is justified.

The band members walk over to look at Eva's design. Their faces don't reveal anything, and I hold my breath as they walk over to my easel.

"Well, well, well," Theo says. "Isn't this *fascinating*?"

"There's a clear winner here, don't you think?" Chad says.

"Oh, most definitely," Tom agrees.

"No doubt about it," Jimmy says.

Please let it be me. Please, PLEASE, let it be me!

Theo walks back to center stage, and the cameras move in for close-ups of both Eva and me. Great. If Eva wins, I won't have to worry about millions of people seeing my huge zit, because they'll be too busy watching my total and complete misery and humiliation.

"Please turn the easels to the audience," Theo says.

Tom does another drumroll, and as our designs are revealed to the audience, there's a collective gasp.

The moment I see Eva's design, I understand why. To say it's basic is an insult to basicness. It's pretty much a rectangle with clumsily drawn laces and a smaller rectangle for a heel. There's nothing that ties it to the lyrics of "A Million Miles to the Nearest Star."

"Syncos in this auditorium and around the world . . . I think it's pretty clear who is telling the truth and who stole the designs, don't you?" Theo says, giving Eva a dirty look over his shoulder as he walks in my direction. "Congratulations to Araminta Robicheaux! Not only do you have a bright future ahead of you as a shoe designer, but you and a limo full of your closest friends will be getting the VIP treatment at tonight's show!"

"You did it, Minty!" Dad shouts, and I hear the aunties hooting in victory.

Then Ms. Amara joins Mr. Hamilton onstage with the design I did for Chad Apollo's shoes in Couture Club. "Minty designed these shoes—I watched her do it," she says. "I only just found this in my classroom, or I would have brought it up as proof sooner. It was with other fantastic designs our Couture Club students did at the last meeting that I've been meaning to display in the classroom, but haven't had time to hang."

Theo waves Ray the bodyguard over, and then he takes another sheet out of the black briefcase. When he turns it around, it matches my drawing of Chad Apollo's shoes exactly.

"Well, that settles it," Theo says. "Without a reasonable doubt."

Eva stomps off the stage, and a few minutes later I see her march out of the auditorium with her father and his entourage.

I get to take selfies with all the members of the band, including Theo Downey. As he puts his leather jacket-clad arm around me, I wonder if I should confess about the Snowball poop, but only for a second. Some things are better left unsaid.

Mr. Hamilton invites my parents and the aunties up onstage to join me. When Theo Downey sees my aunts, his eyes almost bug out of his head.

"Hold the phone—you're the Comfortably Ever After ladies!" he exclaims.

"That we are, handsome!" Aunt Margaux gives him a big grin. Aunt Lottie blushes and bats her eyelashes.

"You ladies are the best thing on television!" he exclaims. Then, to my amazement and the aunties' delight, Theo and the rest of the band start singing a medley of Comfortably Ever After™ ads, in four-part harmony.

I cannot believe this. All this time that I've been a fan of Retro of Sync, they've been fans of Aunt Margaux and Aunt Lottie.

Every time I think I've started to figure out the world, something like this happens and I realize how much I still have to learn. But one thing I know for sure—I'm going to see Retro of Sync! Suddenly I'm feeling a lot better about this move to New York.

Chapter Thirteen

AFTER THE DRAW-OFF, I GO TO MARIO'S for a celebratory pizza with my friends, telling my parents and the aunties I'll meet them back at the apartment. When I get home, the apartment smells of heavenly baked goods. I find Mom in the kitchen with Aunt Margaux, who is removing a tray of perfectly golden oatmeal raisin cookies from the oven. Not a single one is burned, and there's no smoke in the kitchen.

I grab one from the pile already on the cooling rack and taste it. It practically melts in my mouth.

"Aunt Margaux, these are amazing!" I say. "See, you can cook!"

"Well, I can't take all the credit," Margaux says. "Ella supervised."

"And I didn't even have to dial 911," Aunt Lottie teases as she comes into the kitchen. "It's a miracle!"

Aunt Margaux scowls at her, but Aunt Lottie just smiles and helps herself to a cookie.

"So, have you decided who you want to take to the concert?" Mom asks, pouring herself a cup of tea.

I finish my cookie before answering. "I asked Aria, her friend Jesse, Sophie, Nina, Livvy, and Dakota—"

"Oooh, Minty's crush!" Aunt Lottie shrieks.

Mom chokes on her spit.

"Crush? What crush? I've been away less than a week and I missed my daughter's first crush?"

"You snooze, you lose, Ella dear," Aunt Lottie says with a little too much glee.

Mom collapses into a chair, apparently knocked over by the fact that her only daughter, who she left at home while she pursued World Cleaning Product Domination, dared to develop a crush *while she was gone.*

"Here, have a cookie, Ella. You look like you need the sugar," Aunt Margaux says, shoving one in Mom's face.

Mom actually starts eating it, and I use the opportunity to tell them the last four people I want to come.

"I was also thinking that you and Dad and the aunties should come. Since none of this would have happened without you going to Europe and leaving me with Margaux and Lottie."

This seems to come as a shock to the aunties, because they collapse into chairs on either side of Mom.

"Here, have a cookie," I say, giving one to each of them. "You look like you need the sugar."

To my horror, they both burst into tears and start crying loudly. To my even greater horror, Mom joins them.

"What is going on?" Dad runs into the kitchen, apparently alerted by the sobbing. "I thought we were celebrating." Then he spots the cookies and grabs one in each hand. "Wow, these are *sooooo* good."

That makes Aunt Margaux cry even more.

Dad and I give each other a *what is even happening* look.

"You don't have to come if you don't want to," I say. "I just thought—"

"Of c-course we want to," Aunt Lottie sniffs, standing up and clasping me to her soggy bosom.

"We d-didn't think you'd w-want us," Aunt Margaux says, grabbing a handful of kitchen towel and blowing her nose loudly. "Because we embarrass you."

The truth is, if you'd asked me on Monday when we

were filming the commercial if I'd want to go to a *Retro of Sync* concert with the aunties, it would have been a hard no. But as it turns out, what Mom said before she left was right. I have learned a lot from the aunties this week, once I started being more open to them. Maybe the most important thing is how much they love me.

"Oh, please," I say. "You can't possibly embarrass me more than Mom and Dad."

Dad spits out his cookie crumbs all over the counter.

"See what I mean?" I say.

The aunties go from soggy sniffs to riotous guffaws. Even Mom gives me a watery smile.

"Marge, I think we should give her the surprise," Aunt Lottie says.

"Good thinking," Aunt Margaux says, rushing out of the room without even reminding Aunt Lottie not to call her Marge.

Dad wipes the spewed cookie crumbs off the counter. "Ella, I think I got some in Lottie's hair—can you pick them out for her?"

Mom is removing the crumbs when Aunt Margaux comes back with a large silver bag.

Aunt Margaux hands it to me. "Here you go, Minty darling."

Inside the bag is a Comfortably Ever After™ shoebox, tied up with a silver bow. My heart sinks. Even if it's the ugliest pair of shoes in the universe, I'm going to have to pretend I love them, put them on, and wear them to the concert. I don't want to hurt the aunties' feelings, especially after everything they've done for me.

"Go on, open it!" Aunt Lottie says.

My fingers tremble as I pull the bow undone and open the box, expecting the worst. But inside is a pair of totally awesome sneakers.

It takes me a second or two to recognize the design. It's one of mine.

"Wait—that looks like one of my—how did you?" I stammer.

"I snuck a picture of your practice designs," Aunt Margaux says.

"We loved them," Aunt Lottie says. "So we got our shoemaker to hand-make a prototype. Once we negotiate with you for the design, we want to make this one of the representative shoes for our Comfortably Ever After for Youth line."

I slide the shoes on and tie the laces. My feet feel like they're singing hallelujah. These are the most comfortable shoes I've ever worn.

"It's like wearing clouds on my feet," I say.

"'It feels like I'm wearing clouds on my feet . . . ,'" Aunt Lottie repeats slowly. "That's a great tagline. Better than some of the ones we've paid our ad agency big bucks for. Can we use that in our next ad?"

"Yes!" Aunt Margaux exclaims. "We could shoot a spot with you in it!"

As much as I'm terrified of the idea after my performance in the last ad, I figure given all the trouble I've caused my aunties, it's the least I can do.

"O . . . kay," I agree. "As long as I don't have to dance or rap."

"Especially not at the same time," Aunt Lottie says, with a twinkle in her eyes.

"Deal!" Aunt Margaux says.

"Wait, you said negotiate for the use of the design," I say. "So I'm going to get a percentage of the profits, right?"

My parents and the aunties look at one another. They're all smiling.

"That's my girl," Aunt Lottie says, beaming.

"No, she's my girl," Aunt Margaux says.

"Technically, she's *my* girl," Mom points out.

"Eh-hem. She's *our* girl," Dad argues.

"I'm my *own* girl," I state loudly and firmly, before

heading to my room to figure out what I'm going to wear with my fab new sneakers tomorrow when we go to the concert.

That evening, I'm just finishing tying the glittery laces on my Comfortably Ever After™ sneakers when the doorbell rings.

"I'll get it!" I shout, but I trip on my untied lace and Dad gets there first.

This is not good. He and Mom have been acting strangely freaked out about the crush news. They've been trying to interrogate me about Dakota all afternoon. I finally pointed out that Dad decided he was *soooooooooooo* in love with Mom *without even knowing her name*. My parents didn't find that little reminder nearly as amusing as the aunties did, but at least it shut them up.

My friends file into the apartment. Dad glares at both the guys and asks: "Which one of you is Dakota?"

"Robbie . . . you promised," Mom says in a warning tone.

Dad lifts a princely eyebrow at her.

Dakota shifts on his feet and then takes off the wool beanie that I've never seen him without. He's got really nice hair hidden away under it.

"I am, sir," he says. Then he remembers who my dad is. "I mean, Sir Prince. I mean, your Princely Highness, sir."

"Just call him Mr. Robicheaux," I say. "Mr. R will do."

My father looks at me with a pained expression. "No. It won't."

"Fine, Mr. Robicheaux it is," I tell my friends.

"Wow, where did you get those shoes?" Aria says. "They're amazing."

Nina stares at them, her brow furrowed. "Wait . . . isn't that—"

"My design. Yes it is!" I say. "The aunties had them made!"

"So cool," Livvy says.

Dad's phone rings. He answers it without taking his glaring focus off Dakota.

"We'll be down in a minute," he says, and then hangs up. "Lottie, Margaux, time to go! The limo is here."

I've been nervous about what the aunties plan to wear, but they're actually pretty toned down. Aunt Lottie is sporting leopard-print pants and a black T-shirt that says SYNC-O-PATH. Aunt Margaux is wearing a pair of purple leather trousers with a white T-shirt that says I'M RETRO—DO YOU SYNC? They're both wearing Comfortably Ever After™ shoes based on my designs—

Lottie the Jimmy Strage, and Margaux the Chad Apollo.

"Those are amazing shoes," Nina says.

"They're Minty's designs," Aunt Lottie says.

"We're going into business with her," Aunt Margaux says. "The girl has talent!"

I realize how lucky I am to have aunties in the shoe business. There's no way I would be able to get a licensing deal at my age without having that connection. I don't want to take it for granted and end up behaving like Eva.

"Could we make setting up a scholarship for people who want to be designers but don't have family in the business part of my deal?" I ask. "I bet there are lots of great designers out there who aren't lucky enough to have the kind of connections I do. Don't they deserve a chance too?"

Aunt Margaux strokes her chin. "That's not a bad idea, Minty."

"Yes . . . it would give us a pipeline of interesting young designers so we can appeal to the youths," Aunt Lottie agrees.

"Done!" Margaux says, clapping me on the shoulder so hard I stumble into Dakota, who catches me in his arms, earning himself a "heh-hem" from Dad, who earns himself another "Robbie, you promised" from Mom.

When we're all comfortably seated in the limo, Aria suddenly exclaims, "Did you hear what happened with Eva?"

"No . . . what?" I ask.

"She was going to be expelled for cheating at the contest and stealing your notebook and lying about the designs, because it broke the school's honor code," Aria says. "But her dad made a big donation and so she's just getting a week's suspension."

"Wow," I say. "Mr. Hamilton really *is* open to persuasion for a big enough check. He must be really happy about all the trouble that's happened since I showed up at MWTMS."

"Ginny Krulinsky told me Eva's complaining because her parents took her credit cards away as punishment," Livvy says. "And she lost her influencer deal with Seiyariyashi Tomaki because he doesn't want his brand to be associated with cheating and dishonesty."

"I'm glad she's having to face some consequences, at least," Aunt Margaux says.

"Otherwise she'll never learn," Mom says.

I realize that I learned from the consequences of making an unclear wish, and I send a silent thank-you to Leila and Goldenbreast. My wishes are coming true after all.

Even though there's a chill in the air, we ask Tariq, the limo driver, to open the sunroof so we can look up at the stars. He puts on Retro of Sync's latest album, and we sing along as we drive through Central Park to the West Side and then down to the Garden.

Our VIP box at Madison Square Garden is unbelievable. There's a sideboard loaded with food and a refrigerator loaded with drinks. Best of all, we have a great view.

Then the lights dim, and the band walks out onstage.

"Helloooo, New York City!" Theo says, and the place goes wild.

But I'm busy looking at their feet. Because it looks like . . .

"We'd like to welcome our special guest—the winner of our shoe-design contest, a very talented student, Miss Minty Robicheaux!"

The next thing I know, my shocked face is on the jumbotrons on the either side of the stage. The zit on my chin is the size of a small continent, which makes me want to cover it with my hands, but the entire arena is cheering, which is . . . kind of amazing. Am I a terrible person for thinking how jealous Eva must be, wherever she's sitting?

"And thanks to the lovely ladies of Comfortably Ever After, Lottie and Margaux, for having Minty's designs rush-made into these incredibly comfortable shoes," Theo continues.

He jumps up and down like the shoes give him extra energy.

Then the band launches into "Life in the Big City," which of course makes the New York crowd go wild.

My friends and I are dancing to the beat and my parents are dancing with the aunties in a way that makes me glad the camera isn't pointed in our direction anymore.

The shoes the aunties made from my design are cushioning my feet, and I'm so happy it feels like I'm dancing on air.

I've gotten everything I wished for—and more.

Acknowledgments

THANK YOU TO THE TEAM AT SIMON & Schuster/Aladdin—Mara Anastas, Fiona Simpson, Laura Lyn DiSiena, Angela Navarra, Rebecca Vitkus, Karen Sherman, Kayley Hoffman, and most especially my delightful editor, Alyson Heller. I'm so grateful to have the opportunity to look at the fairy tales that I was brought up with way back when, and riff on them with twenty-first-century eyes for a new generation.

To my beloved agent, Jennifer Laughran, I send love, hugs, and adorable sloths. Also puppies. Lots of very cute puppies.

I'm grateful to all the friends who chimed in on Facebook when I asked a legal question about recording someone without their knowledge in New York State. Amy D'Amico, Mel Issa Norris, Shari Deutsch, Leah Cypess, Stephanie Gorin, Steve Hart, Harold Underdown, Sara Reed Houldcroft, and Matt Waggoner, that spirited conversation made me wish I'd gone to law school instead of business school. Y'all rock!

My fellow Swingers of Birches and Sisters of the Brass Necklace—thank you for helping to provide sanity and sisterhood in a crazy-making world.

I'm so proud of my children, Josh and Amie, for the adults they have become. Mama's kvelling, and now you have it in writing.

Last—but not ever least—my love and deepest gratitude to my husband, Hank, for putting up with the crazy symptoms of my incredibly stressful 2018 writing life, and most especially for the trip to Bonaire while I was working on revisions for this book. Prince Charming's got nothing on you, babe.

Looking for another great book?
Find it
IN THE MIDDLE.

Fun, fantastic books for kids
in the in-be**TWEEN** age.

IntheMiddleBooks.com

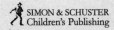 

Be sure to m!x it up by catching up on the latest drama!